ROYAL DANGER

THE MYSTIQUE SERIES
BOOK 2

AVISHAI EL

AVI

CONTENTS

1

———

VAUGHAN'S DISAPPEARANCE

Flower's body trembled as she sat on the cold floor, each breath coming in short, ragged gasps. The weight of the guilt crushed her, and her mind swirled with memories of the warnings—the cryptic visions that had haunted her for so long. She had been entrusted with Vaughan's safety, told over and over to protect her, but somehow, she had failed. It wasn't just a warning; it was a responsibility—one she had let slip through her fingers.

Why didn't I act sooner? The question echoed in her mind. Vivid images of Andres flashed through her thoughts: his smiling face, his trusting eyes, and the way he had died so suddenly, so violently. The sharp memory of his lifeless body still haunted her dreams. Could she have saved him? No, but the feeling of regret overwhelmed her.

Her heart ached with the familiar sting of loss, of failure. She frantically looked at her phone for any sign of Vaughan, but all she saw was the silent screen, the unanswered call. Her thoughts twisted, each one more unbearable than the last. *What if this is it? What if it's too late?*

The shrill, agonizing cry that had erupted from her lungs felt like it might tear her apart. She clutched her chest, but the sobs came in waves.

I swore I wouldn't fail her. The thought was like a dagger lodged deep in her chest. But no matter how much she begged and blamed herself, it didn't change the fact that Vaughan was out there—alone and in danger.

The world outside seemed so far away now, as if she were trapped in an endless fog. Yet somewhere deep within, a spark of determination flickered.

She wiped her tears away, her fingers shaking but resolute. She had to find Vaughan. She couldn't fail her again.

Flower's heart pounded in her chest as she faced the man standing before her, his hand gripping the gleaming knife with a tight, almost practiced hold. The rage in his eyes made her shiver, but she couldn't let it paralyze her. Vaughan was still in that building.

She darted left, then right, trying to find an opening, but he was too quick. Every move she made, he mirrored it, trapping her in a corner. Her breath came in ragged gasps as she tried to figure out how to break free. The cold, hard floor beneath her felt like it was closing in.

Then, she stumbled.

Her foot collided with something heavy, sending it crashing to the ground. The sound of metal clanging against stone resounded through the room, and as her eyes darted down, she saw it—a pan, ancient and worn, its surface etched with symbols that seemed to dance in the dim light.

Vaughan's gaze fixed on the symbols, and the world around her blurred. It was as though her mind was slipping into a strange, dreamlike fog where nothing felt real, yet everything was vivid. The symbols—ancient, otherworldly—pulled her in, whispered something she couldn't quite understand, but she felt it deep in her bones.

Snap out of it. She shook her head. Her eyes widened, trying to regain focus. She could hear the man's footsteps coming closer, his breath heavy with anger. Fear clawed at her insides, but she was not going to let him do this to her.

With a surge of adrenaline, Vaughan broke free from the trance. She sprang to her feet, her mind clearing, and in one swift motion, she charged at the man, her hands finding the pan she had just knocked over. She swung it with all her strength, connecting hard with his skull.

The man staggered back, grunting in pain. For a brief moment, his grip on the knife loosened, and Vaughan took advantage of the opening. Her pulse raced, but there was no time to hesitate.

Vaughan's breath came in ragged bursts as she quickly burst through the gas station doors. In the dimly lit room, her words tumbled out in a torrent. The gas station clerk, a teenager with tired eyes, glanced at her over the counter, seeming unsure how to respond. She wiped the sweat from her brow with the back of her hand, her palms clammy. People in the station murmured, exchanging uncertain glances.

But Vaughan wasn't crazy. At least, not in the way they thought. Her hands trembled as she gripped the edge of the counter. All she wanted was someone to pull her back and believe her.

"Please," she said, her voice raw, "he's coming. I don't know how long I have, but I—I need help. He won't stop until—"

The clerk looked at her skeptically, then with thinly veiled concern. He picked up the phone, but something in his eyes revealed he wasn't fully convinced.

"He's got a knife," she added, forcing herself to sound clear. "He's not going to stop. Please, you have to call the police." Desperation pulled at her voice like a string about to snap.

A woman in the corner, sitting with her coffee, muttered under her breath, "Another one of those cases—"

"Shut up!"

The woman looked offended and shocked, placing her hand over her chest as she turned away.

Vaughan may have been afraid, but she never tolerated disrespect.

Her heart pounded in her chest, reminding her the clock was ticking. She stood there waiting to see if the gas station clerk would actually call the police, hoping someone would believe her before it was too late,

He was out there. And he was coming.

Meanwhile, on the other side of town, Flower had an unsettling vision that left her with an uneasy feeling in her chest. She could see Vaughan in her mind, but not in the way she usually did. This time, she saw her restless, confused—something was wrong. Flower had always been able to sense other people's emotions, but this time, it was different. Vaughan wasn't just lost in thought; she was lost in a way Flower had never felt before.

As the phone rang, Flower's thoughts returned to the gas station. She wondered if Vaughan had gotten into some sort of trouble, or if the situation had escalated more than she could've imagined. "Please, let them find her," Flower whispered, hoping her gut feeling wasn't leading her astray.

When the police answered, Flower quickly explained everything —how she saw Vaughan, the feeling of urgency, and the possible danger she was in. "I need your help," Flower said, her voice tight. "You have to find her."

Flower tried to steady her breath. She had done what she could; now all she could do was wait. The unknown stretched before her like a dark, looming tunnel. Would they find Vaughan before it was too late?

As Vaughan stood, trembling and fighting the surge of emotions threatening to overwhelm her, the world around her seemed to fade.

But she could see the gas station clerk eyeing her with suspicion, shaking his head. He hung up the phone.

She tussled with the tears that wanted to roll down her face like a slow waterfall. It swiftly turned into anger until her mind drifted into a vision, her mother's voice echoing softly in the distance. It was a voice of worry, tinged with love and concern—a voice she hadn't heard in far too long.

In the vision, Vaughan saw her mother pacing the floor of their old house, phone pressed to her ear. "Please, please be safe." Her mother's words broke through the veil of her thoughts. Her mother's eyes were wide, brows furrowed, and every inch of her body seemed tense. It was the kind of worry only a mother could feel—a worry that knew no distance.

Vaughan snapped back to the present, the shaking in her hands subsiding as her heart steadied, her anger morphing into something clearer, more focused. She realized that her mother was already doing everything she could, and in that moment, Vaughan knew she couldn't let her own fears control her any longer.

The gas station clerk, still eyeing her suspiciously, didn't seem to understand the gravity of the situation. He probably just thought she was some erratic woman, lost in her own paranoia. But Vaughan was beyond the need for validation. She had her mission.

She pulled her coat tighter around her body and stepped back a little. Then she glanced at the door, almost willing the police to show up faster, but she knew better than to rush them. If she had learned anything over the years, it was that everything happened in its own time. The wait, as uncomfortable as it was, was a part of the process —just like the visions.

Vaughan let out a slow, steadying breath, closing her eyes for a moment. Her mind was still racing, but she felt her connection to Flower's intention, her mother's call, and the quiet strength inside her that had been buried under the chaos of recent events.

The world seemed to move around her, each second dragging on as she waited.

Vaughan lay there, barely conscious, her breath shallow. The noise of the gas station, the hum of engines, and the faint chatter of customers felt distant, as though they were happening in another world. Her vision blurred, and her body grew colder with each minute.

People came and went, oblivious to her presence. The gas station clerk, stationed behind the counter, stole occasional glances but never approached. The world outside the glass windows seemed busy, but inside, there was a suffocating indifference.

Vaughan's mind swirled in and out of focus as her strength wavered. *Why is this happening? Why won't anyone help?*

After what seemed like an eternity, the sirens resounded in the distance. They grew louder, but the time seemed to stretch on impossibly long. Finally, the police officers rushed in, their boots loud on the floor, their voices frenzied.

"Where is she? Where is Vaughan?" one of them shouted, scanning the gas station.

The gas station clerk, his face pale, finally spoke shakily. "I-I had no idea . . . I didn't see anything . . . Please . . . don't get me in trouble." His hands trembled as he wiped his forehead.

The officers exchanged looks of disbelief. They had expected something different—a more proactive response from those nearby. But it seemed the clerk's lack of attention, his inability to recognize the gravity of the situation, was just another symptom of the coldness that had taken over this place.

Vaughan's eyes fluttered open one last time, the presence of the officers slowly pulling her from the fog. Would she ever feel seen again?

They wheeled Vaughan toward the ambulance, her limbs limp under the emergency blankets, her skin pale as porcelain under the streetlights. A thin oxygen mask fogged with her shallow.

She didn't move. Didn't speak.

Onlookers watched in silence as the paramedics loaded her in, one of them already prepping an IV, the other shouting vitals into the radio.

"She's crashing," someone muttered.

One of the paramedics leaned toward the officers, her voice tight. "She's fading fast. They don't think she'll make it to the hospital."

Meanwhile Vaughan slipped into a vision. She saw him—a figure cloaked in shimmering gold, as if carved from the very metal itself. He was aged, regal, and still. His voice echoed like thunder wrapped in velvet.

"Child . . . do you even know who you are?"

Then, the figure was disrupted and overshadowed by the man.

The glint of the knife. The wet shine of blood on the blade. His eyes—familiar, cold, unforgiving. It was him.

Back in the real world, machines hummed as Vaughan's vitals plunged.

"We're losing her!" a paramedic shouted.

But Vaughan was already falling—into darkness, or memory. Or something worse.

Back at home, Flower could sense that Vaughan was in a safe place, though she hadn't heard from the officers.

But it wasn't logical. It wasn't from ashwagandha or fatigue. It was something more primal, as though something inside her knew that Vaughan—despite all evidence—was not only alive but . . . protected.

She paced back and forth when she heard it—a low, raspy groan that floated through the walls like a draft. It was the sound of an old man straining for attention. The familiarity of it froze her mid-step. It reminded her of the strange encounter from her childhood—the man who had startled her without a word, just a look, and then vanished.

To her surprise, she flinched again, the memory crawling up her spine. And then irritation followed. *Really? Now?* Of all times, a ghost decided to make an appearance.

What does he want? she thought bitterly. *Can he not sense I'm not in the mood for haunting right now? I'm worried about my daughter, and he chooses now?*

Frustrated, she snapped, "What do you want?"

The air bent slightly, a shimmer in the dim hallway light, and there he was. The same unkempt hair. The same scuffed black shoes. No older.

He looked at her without blinking, and his voice echoed in her head, not in her ears.

"Vaughan may be fine . . . but she needs you now."

She looked at him, eyes narrowing—how did he know? What exactly did he know? And why did Vaughan need her?

Before she could speak, the phone rang.

She glanced at it, then back at the man, questions burning behind her gaze. Why her? What was so urgent? But maybe it *was* an emergency. She picked up the phone.

It was the doctor from the hospital.

His voice crackled through the phone, clinical yet strained. "Vaughan has slipped into a coma. She's unresponsive . . . but we believe she may wake within two to four days."

No cardiac arrest. No clear cause. Just an unexplained darkness that baffled the doctors and left Flower's heart pounding.

The phone slipped from her trembling hand. Her knees gave out, and she slid down the door, sobbing. Vaughan was fighting for her life, and Flower wasn't there to protect her.

Failure wrapped its cold fingers around her mind, whispering the same thoughts she'd buried before: *You weren't enough. You weren't there when it mattered.*

For a moment, she couldn't breathe. Couldn't think. All she could do was drown in the helpless tears streaming down her face—tears that burned with guilt, fear, and the unshakable feeling that something far more sinister was at play.

Flower wiped her tear-streaked face, forcing herself to breathe. She didn't have the luxury of falling apart—not now. Vaughan needed her. Somewhere deep inside, a single thought burned like a command: *Go to her. Now.*

She grabbed her purse, snatched up her phone and keys, and bolted out the door. The night air was thick and almost electric, as if it knew something she didn't. Sliding into the driver's seat, she jammed the keys into the ignition, and the engine roared to life.

The streets were nearly empty, bathed in the cold glow of street-lights. Her knuckles whitened around the steering wheel as she sped through the silence, careful not to drive recklessly.

As she switched lanes, her headlights put a spotlight on a figure—a man in a black coat, wearing a tall, antiquated top hat. The same man she'd seen before. Her stomach dropped.

Before she could blink, the distance between them vanished in an instant. Then he was sitting in her backseat. His voice slithered into her ears, low and almost mocking, though his lips never moved.

"You know those doctors think Vaughan is in a coma," he said, his tone chilling, "but she's not. She's trapped in visions. Another realm. And I decide what happens next."

Her chest tightened. Flower gripped the steering wheel so hard it hurt, eyes darting back to the road. When she looked in her mirror again, the man was gone, as if he had melted into the night.

The hospital came into view like a beacon and a warning all at once. She parked haphazardly and sprinted through the glass doors, ignoring the questioning looks of the night staff. The corridors stretched on endlessly, the fluorescent lights buzzing overhead. Every step seemed louder than the last.

She burst into Vaughan's room. Machines beeped in a steady rhythm. Vaughan lay motionless, her skin pale against the stark white sheets. Flower sank into the chair beside the bed, her fingers brushing her daughter's cold hand.

"I'm here, baby," she whispered. "I'm not leaving you."

Hours crawled by. Doctors came and went, their faces careful masks of professionalism that barely hid their confusion. They spoke of tests, brain activity, medical definitions—but none of it explained the fear that clung to the room.

Flower barely slept. She dozed in the chair, clutching Vaughan's hand. When she closed her eyes, she saw flashes of the man with the top hat—standing at the foot of the bed, his shadow stretching impossibly long, his knife glinting under the dim hospital light. She would jolt awake only to find the room empty.

~

Two days passed. On the third morning, as the sun cast a fragile light through the blinds, something changed. Vaughan's fingers twitched. Her eyelids fluttered open, revealing eyes glassy with tears but filled with recognition. A weak smile spread across her face.

"Mom . . ."

Flower held her daughter as she sobbed. The reunion was raw, messy, and beautiful. They held onto each other as if the world would disappear if they let go.

Doctors kept Vaughan for observation, insisting on two more days to ensure she was stable. Flower stayed by her side, refusing to leave her alone for even a second.

That night, Vaughan fell into a restless sleep. Her breathing hitched, her head twitching violently against the pillow. Flower stirred, reaching out, but before she could wake her, Vaughan stiffened. Her body was trapped in something unseen. Her chest rose and fell rapidly, sweat forming on her brow.

In her dream, the man in the black coat stood closer than ever, the brim of his hat casting a shadow over eyes that glowed unnaturally. A glinting knife flashed in his hand as he stepped closer. His voice was a growl, each word dripping with malice.

"You better listen," he snarled, "or this ends now."

The heart monitor spiked, beeping erratically. Alarms blared. Nurses and doctors rushed in, snapping Flower from her own restless sleep. She bolted upright, eyes darting to her daughter.

Vaughan's eyes flew open. She screamed, her voice cracking. "There's a man! He's coming! You have to help me!"

The staff restrained her gently, trying to calm her, but Flower knew—this wasn't just a nightmare. The man was real. He was coming. And whatever he wanted, he wouldn't stop until he got it.

For the next forty-eight hours, paranoia hung in the air like smoke. Flower noticed shadows where there shouldn't be any. The nurses whispered outside the door, their voices sharp with concern. Even the security cameras in the hall seemed to flicker when no one was watching.

Whenever Vaughan closed her eyes, she twitched, murmuring under her breath. Flower tried to decipher the words, leaning close, only catching fragments: *knife . . . dark . . . can't run . . . he knows . . .*

On the second night of observation, Flower sat awake with the small hospital lamp casting a weak glow. She thought she saw movement in the corner of the room—a ripple in the air, like heat rising from asphalt. She blinked, and the man stood there, his knife dangling lazily in his grip, his smile razor-sharp.

"You can't keep her safe," he hissed. "Not from what's coming."

Before Flower could scream, the lights flickered violently, filling the room with darkness. The heart monitor shrieked, its pitch deafening. Nurses stormed in, but the man was gone, leaving only the cold scent of smoke.

When the lights returned, Vaughan was gasping, her eyes wild. "He's coming for both of us," she whispered hoarsely, clutching her mother's hand. "Mom, you have to believe me. He's real."

Flower held her tight, her own voice trembling but fierce. "I believe you. And I'll do whatever it takes to stop him."

Outside the room, unseen, the man with the top hat lingered in the reflection of the hospital window. His presence was not physical, but it was there—dark, menacing, undeniable. The glass distorted his face, stretching his grin impossibly wide, as if the very act of watching them brought him joy. The night cloaked him, and as dawn crept over the horizon, he faded.

By morning, the room buzzed with sterile light and hushed voices. The nurse entered with the doctor, their expressions professional but tinged with curiosity. Behind them, two uniformed officers followed, their radios crackling softly. One of them, a tall man with a weathered face, spoke gently.

"We need to ask you a few questions, Vaughan. Just to understand what happened now that you're awake."

Vaughan sat upright, clutching the thin hospital blanket around her shoulders. Her voice trembled, but her eyes—still clouded with fear—met theirs. "There was a man. He came after me with a knife. I don't know why. I ran, but he. . . kept coming. I don't know what he wants with me."

The officers leaned closer, jotting down her words. She hesitated, the truth itching at the edge of her tongue. *Should I tell them everything?* The visions, the whispers in her sleep, the way he existed beyond dreams—it all swirled inside her chest. But she knew better. People twist what they fear. She had embraced her psychic gifts in secret, but this was not the time to reveal them.

She kept it simple, omitting the visions and the warnings that had haunted her. The officers promised increased patrols, but their sidelong glances said they thought this was just stress.

After the questioning, doctors cleared her to leave, though they couldn't explain the coma. Flower clung to Vaughan as they walked into the sunlight, determined to shield her daughter from whatever darkness followed them.

Back at Flower's home, the walls felt safe, wrapped in lavender and quiet prayers Flower murmured when she thought Vaughan was asleep. Over tea, Vaughan spilled the truth she had hidden from the officers—the visions, the man, how he came to her in places beyond logic. Flower listened, pale but unwavering. "You're safe here," she said, gripping her hand. "As long as you're with me, he can't touch you."

The house became a sanctuary, yet the visions didn't stop. Each night, Vaughan dreamed of game shows—blinding lights, cheering crowds. She stood on stage, smiling nervously. *You're up. You're it.* The voices would chant as the lights died, and the crowd faded, leaving her stranded in darkness with distant laughter.

Days blurred. She tried to live normally—helping Flower, sipping tea on the porch, and reading. Yet even in daylight, the game show's echo stalked her. Sometimes she swore she saw movement in her periphery—shadows that vanished when she turned her head.

Midweek, her aunt Sunshine arrived like a burst of color. Sunshine's laughter filled the house, her warmth cutting through the gloom. She hugged Vaughan fiercely, showering her with questions and stories, her energy a shield. For hours, the house felt alive, and Vaughan smiled for real. With her aunt's presence, the visions weakened.

By week's end, Vaughan felt stronger. The man hadn't appeared since Sunshine's visit. Hope crept back into her chest. Returning to her own home felt like reclaiming territory. She dressed in white, styled her hair in soft updos. For the first time since the coma, she felt alive.

To celebrate, she visited the new Third Eye Arena Ice Cream Shop. Inside, the scent of vanilla and cinnamon wrapped around her, comforting. She ordered a vegan vanilla cone, savoring its sweetness as she stepped into the sun. For a heartbeat, everything felt perfect. Normal. Safe.

But as she licked the melting ice cream, a faint reflection in the shop's window caught her eye—tall, dark, a glint of a top hat. She blinked. The glass was empty.

She forced a smile, whispering, "He's gone." She was free—or so she thought.

That night, as she drifted to sleep in her own bed, the game show lights flickered back to life. The audience roared. The faceless host grinned. *You're up. You're it.* The stage went black. And somewhere in the shadows, the man's low laughter began again.

When Vaughan woke up, sunlight streamed softly through her curtains, painting the room in shades of gold. For a brief moment, she almost forgot the horrors of the past weeks. But the memory lingered at the edge of her mind. Today, she decided, would be hers. A day to reclaim her strength.

The sound of water filled the bathroom as she ran a hot bath, steam curling around the mirror. The scent of rose body wash rose with the mist. Slipping into the water, she let it wash over her, feeling her muscles loosen under the warmth. She closed her eyes, inhaling deeply. When she finally stepped out, the air was cool against her skin. She wrapped herself in a soft towel.

She brushed her teeth, watching herself in the mirror, determination flickering in her eyes. Her movements were meticulous—each stroke of the brush, each rinse a small ritual of self-care. She tied her hair into a high ponytail, letting a single strand fall across her face in a deliberate sweep. It made her feel strong and fierce like a warrior preparing for battle.

Dressing in comfortable hiking clothes, Vaughan checked her phone. There was a text from Antonio. He'd been checking in on her often since the hospital. When they met a while ago, he gave her a job at the gun range—he'd taught her how to shoot, how to aim, how to defend herself. But she had stopped going. Guns felt heavy now, a reminder of the danger lurking. Still, she appreciated his messages and still kept a gun with her. She typed a quick reply, assuring him she was fine, then slipped her phone into her backpack.

The hike was two hours away, near a stretch of beach lined with small shops and a weathered beach house she had always admired. She planned to make a day of it—hiking, exploring, and maybe letting the ocean remind her that there was beauty left in the world.

The drive was peaceful. Trees lined the highway, swaying gently in the wind. When she arrived, the scent of saltwater greeted her. Waves reminiscent of turquoise green and blue crashed rhythmically against the shore, and gulls cried overhead. The hike began at the edge of the beach, winding through sandy paths that gave way to rocky trails overlooking the ocean.

At a small snack store near the beach, Vaughan stopped for water. The cashier, a cheerful young woman, complimented her hair and chatted warmly. At the gas station, an elderly man struck up a conversation, telling her about the area's history. Everyone seemed kind, open—like the universe was trying to remind her that not every stranger was a threat.

Later, as she sat on a bench eating a granola bar, an older couple approached. They smiled warmly, the woman's eyes sparkling. "You're gorgeous, dear," the woman said. "Are you here alone?" Vaughan smiled politely, thanking them. She kept her answers vague. Something in her gut told her to stay guarded.

As the couple walked away, she felt a shift in the air. From the corner of her eye, she noticed an older woman approaching. Her presence was unsettling and otherworldly. She had sharp features, a long crooked nose, and a gaze that pierced straight through Vaughan. Her hair was wild, gray streaks tangled like a storm.

"How does it feel," the woman rasped, her voice low and cutting, "to go to sleep and see everything?"

The words sliced through Vaughan. The woman's eyes locked onto hers, unblinking as if she could see every secret Vaughan had buried. Unlike the other visions Vaughan had encountered, this woman didn't vanish. She stood there—solid, real.

"Who are you?" Vaughan whispered, but the woman only smirked.

"You know who we are. You've seen us. You've seen *him*." She stepped closer. "They're watching."

Panic rippled through Vaughan, but before she could move, the woman turned and walked away, disappearing into the crowd of beachgoers. Vaughan's hands trembled. This wasn't a vision.

Questions swirled in her mind. Was there a cult after her? Were these visions warnings of something bigger? What did they want from her? And most terrifying of all—what was coming?

The ocean roared louder. Vaughan clutched her backpack, scanning the horizon. The beauty of the day now felt like a facade, masking something dark that lingered just out of sight. The hike continued, but every glance from a stranger seemed suspicious.

By the time she returned to her car, the sun was sinking, staining the sky in hues of red and gold. Vaughan drove home in silence, her mind replaying the woman's words. Sleep would come, but with it, the visions. And maybe, this time, something worse.

The day that began as Vaughan's own had ended with a question: *What do they want?* The answer, she feared, was already waiting for her in her dreams.

Despite the terror curling in her chest, Vaughan had grown strangely accustomed to the chaos shadowing her life. If something —or someone—was after her, she would not give it the satisfaction of seeing her break. So she returned to the beach, not just to reclaim her peace, but to prove to herself that she was stronger.

The late afternoon sun bathed the sand in molten gold, the salty breeze weaving through her hair. Waves rolled lazily to shore, foaming at the edges before retreating back into the endless ocean. Children's laughter floated through the air, mingling with the cries of gulls overhead. Vendors dotted the boardwalk, the scent of fried food and tropical fruits clinging to the wind.

That's when she spotted a man selling fresh fruit drinks out of a small, colorful shack decorated with palm fronds. On impulse, she ordered a nonalcoholic pineapple piña colada, the icy sweetness cooling her from the inside out as she wandered closer to the surf. A few feet away, a little girl caught her attention. No more than four years old, the child danced at the water's edge in a yellow bathing suit, her sleek dark hair tied in a ponytail with bangs framing her tiny face. Her giggles were infectious—bright, pure, and innocent. Watching her, Vaughan felt something loosen in her chest. The laughter lifted her spirit, warming the part of her that had been clenched tight with dread.

The little girl reminded her of herself—tan skin glowing in the sunlight, eyes sparkling with curiosity and fearlessness. Vaughan took it as a sign: She was safe, at least for now. The ominous woman from the day before, the one whose presence had rattled her, was gone.

After the beach, she decided to extend the day, savoring every ounce of normalcy it offered. She drove to the mall, the radio playing "Pocketful of Sunshine" by Natasha Bedingfield. The lyrics washed over her, a perfect soundtrack to the calm blooming in her heart. As the song's chorus soared, she closed her eyes at a stoplight, enjoying the stillness.

The mall was alive with the hum of shoppers. Cool air swept over her as she stepped inside, a sharp contrast to the lingering warmth of the beach. Stores glimmered with summer displays—mannequins clad in bright sundresses, sparkling jewelry, and racks of shoes lined neatly in rows. The faint scent of coffee and freshly baked pretzels mingled in the air. Vaughan purchased a few small items—lip balm, a scarf, a new journal—simple tokens that grounded her in this moment.

When she exited the store, her path led to the mall's central atrium where lush green plants framed a trickling water fountain. People lounged on benches—chatting, scrolling their phones, and sipping on drinks. The water shimmered under the skylight, cascading over smooth stones into a shallow pool. She walked toward the center, taking in the peaceful murmuring.

That's when she saw him.

He stood out instantly, as if the world around them had dimmed to sharpen his edges. She didn't have to think—her body moved first. She speed-walked away, every nerve screaming danger. Her hand fumbled for her phone, desperate to call the police, but before she could dial, he was there.

Right there.

He stood close enough that she could see the reflection of the skylight in his eyes. And in his hand—gleaming under the mall's lights—a knife.

Time slowed. But strangely, she didn't flinch. She didn't scream.

Maybe this was it. She had done the work, she told herself. If this was how it ended, she would meet it with grace. She thought of the laughter of the little girl at the beach, the sunlight on the water, and let the memory fill her.

Calmly, she slipped her phone out of her pocket. With her fingers steady despite the adrenaline coursing through her, she sent a single text to her mother: *I love you.*

The man's hand trembled slightly as he looked at the knife, then at her face. Her calmness seemed to unnerve him. She stood rooted, her gaze unwavering.

He exhaled, the tension in his shoulders visible. Slowly, he lowered the knife and slid it back into his coat.

"I'm sorry to startle you," he said, voice low, almost regretful. "I need to use this."

Vaughan's body remained taut, ready to spring at any moment, but she said nothing. Her spirit whispered to her: *Stay quiet. Let him reveal the truth.*

He took a cautious step closer. "You need to come with me."

Still, she did not speak. Her eyes locked on his, unblinking, daring him to explain himself.

Minutes passed in charged stillness before he continued, words falling like stones into the quiet. "You don't know what's coming for you. I'm not here to hurt you—I'm here because they will."

She kept her lips sealed. Her instincts told her to listen, to absorb every word.

"They sent me," he said. "But I'm not doing this their way. You're coming with me because if you don't, they'll find you here and you won't walk away next time."

A vision flashed before her eyes—blinding white light and a figure whispering, *Go with him.* It was as if the universe itself nudged her forward. Even then, she didn't speak. She simply nodded once, barely perceptible, and took a single step toward him.

The mall's background noise faded. The fountain's murmur became a distant echo. All she heard was the low hum of something greater guiding her.

Finally, she broke the silence. "Who are they?"

He met her gaze, a flicker of something—fear?—in his eyes. "You'll see soon enough. But if you want to live, you have to trust me."

2

———

THIS MYSTERIOUS STRANGER

Vaughan slid into the passenger seat, her pulse drumming in her ears. As the door clicked shut, the world outside seemed to vanish. The man gripped the steering wheel, his eyes fixed on the road ahead. She barely trusted him—how could she? Minutes ago, he had come at her with a knife. The air inside the car smelled faintly of leather and rain, a strange comfort amid the tension.

The road unwound before them under a fading sky that bled into streaks of gold and indigo. Fields dotted with wildflowers rolled past, giving way to thick stretches of pine and cedar that climbed steep hills. In the distance, mountains rose like jagged shadows, their snowcaps glowing in the last light of day. Each curve of the road felt like a passage into another world.

The hum of the engine filled the void between them. Questions swirled in Vaughan's mind, clawing for release. Who was he? What was his name? How did he know her, where to find her, and why her of all people?

Finally, she asked, voice low and edged with defiance. "Who are you?"

He didn't look at her. "My name's Eli." His tone carried both weight and secrecy. "I'm not your enemy, Vaughan. If I wanted to hurt you, you wouldn't be here right now."

"And yet you pulled a knife on me," she snapped, her arms folded tightly.

"I had to," he said, eyes never leaving the road. "I needed to see how you'd react. If you'd run, if you'd fight, if you'd listen. You stayed. That told me what I needed to know."

As miles passed, she opened up in ways she didn't expect. She told him about the strange dreams that haunted her, the encounters that left her shaken, and the shadows she felt creeping at the edge of her life. She confessed her fear of losing control, of becoming like the people who had hurt her. For the first time in a long time, she spoke about Flower— the love, the tension—and how much she wished things were simpler.

Eli listened without judgment, offering pieces of himself in return. He revealed he was raised by a secretive group known as the Defiance, trained to protect those born with rare gifts. He spoke of losing his sister to the darkness they now faced, and how every vision since had driven him to prevent the same fate for others. He admitted his psychic gift was both a weapon and a curse: He could see paths but not always change them.

The drive stretched on, weaving through ancient forests where moonlight barely touched the ground. Rivers glinted like spilled mercury in the dark, and fireflies dotted the roadside like tiny lanterns. At one point, a lone deer crossed their path, pausing to stare at them with luminous eyes before vanishing into the trees.

Somewhere along the way, Vaughan dialed Sunshine. Her voice was steady as she gave vague answers about where she was. She didn't call Flower, and that decision festered quietly in the background.

Sunshine's voice was warm, reassuring, almost conspiratorial. "Stay safe, Vaughan. Don't tell anyone where you are yet."

When Flower learned—through Sunshine, not her own daughter —her heart twisted with confusion. Why hadn't Vaughan called her? Why Sunshine? Insecurities flared. Did Vaughan trust Sunshine more? Did she think her sister was more intuitive, more capable of understanding? The thought gnawed at Flower, making her question everything she'd done as a parent.

As they drew closer to their destination, the scenery changed. The trees grew older, thicker, their branches twisting toward the sky as if forming a living cathedral. The air smelled of moss and rain, and Vaughan felt the subtle hum of something ancient beneath the surface. Eli explained that these woods marked the threshold between worlds, a place where the veil was thin.

When they arrived, the place seemed to rise from the earth itself, bathed in an unnatural glow. Ancient trees circled a clearing where a grand hall stood, its walls pulsing faintly as if alive, breathing. The structure shimmered with an iridescence that shifted like the northern lights.

Inside, the scent of burning sage, sandalwood, and lingering smells of vetiver greeted them. Crystal orbs shimmered with shifting colors, each one reflecting fragments of memories and futures. People moved with a quiet purpose, nodding at Eli as they passed.

A massive crystal ball dominated the center of the hall, its surface swirling with clouds of light and shadow. Vaughan felt a pull, as if it was calling to something deep within her. The closer she stepped, the louder the hum in her chest became.

"This," Eli said softly, "is where you'll find answers. And where your real journey begins."

Around them, whispers rose, voices speaking in languages Vaughan didn't recognize yet somehow understood. Every detail—the way the air vibrated, the flicker of unseen energy, the sensation of time bending—confirmed what she already felt. This place was magical, and nothing would ever be the same again.

Vaughan stepped further into the hall, her breath catching as she took in each detail. The crystal ball's glow painted her skin in shifting hues, the light caressing her. Walls of polished stone shimmered faintly, and veins of silver threaded through the floor, pulsing like they carried the Earth's heartbeat. The air vibrated with energy, soft yet powerful. She had never seen, dreamed, or even imagined a place like this.

She whispered to herself, almost afraid to disturb the air. "Why now? Why is this happening now?" Questions pressed in on her, demanding answers. What secrets was it hiding? What did it want from her?

As she stood entranced, her phone vibrated in her pocket. She saw the name—Flower. Her chest tightened. There was mild irritation in her mother's voice the moment she answered. "Vaughan, why didn't you call me first? I had to hear from Sunshine."

Vaughan's throat felt tight. She turned away from the shimmering hall and walked toward a quiet alcove where flickers of light danced against the walls. "Mom, I'm sorry," she said, her voice steady but soft. "I didn't mean to worry you."

Flower's tone softened slightly, but the edge remained. "You didn't mean to, but you did. I'm your mother. I should have been the first to know where you are."

The words sank into Vaughan. She felt the old ache rising—the unspoken feeling that her mother had never truly been there when she needed her most. She had buried that feeling for years. Sunshine had always been easier to talk to, her intuition like an open hand reaching out. Subconsciously, Vaughan had gravitated toward that warmth. She wasn't fully aware of it until now, but it was there. Guilt bloomed in her chest, bitter and cold. She loved her mother, but this truth made her sad in a way words couldn't capture.

She took a deep breath. "Mom, I need you to listen to me carefully. Something happened. I met someone named Elias. He's the reason I'm here, the reason I'm safe."

There was a pause on the other end. "Eli? Who is he?"

"He found me at the mall. At first, he scared me—he had a knife, and I thought he was going to hurt me. But he didn't. He protected me. He . . . he's not like anyone I've ever met. He's psychic, gifted. He says he's a watcher, trained to protect people like me. He's been seeing visions about me, about something dangerous coming."

As she spoke, Eli walked past her quietly, his presence calm and grounding. He moved toward the massive crystal ball, running his fingers over its surface as though he could read its swirling lights. Every so often, he glanced at her with a look that said he understood her unsaid words. He was giving her space, yet his energy enveloped her like a shield.

Flower's voice trembled. "He had a knife, Vaughan? And you got in a car with him?"

"Yes, I got in the car. It felt like the right thing to do, like something was guiding me. We drove for hours. Through mountains, forests, rivers. It was beautiful, Mom. The sky changed colors, and it felt like I was crossing into another world. Elias told me stories about where he's from, about his visions, about how he lost people he loved. He's not a threat, Mom. He's . . . he's here to help me."

There was a long silence on the line. Vaughan could hear her mother's breathing, shaky but controlled. When Flower finally spoke, her voice cracked. "You trusted him more than me."

The words hit Vaughan like a stone to the chest. Tears pricked her eyes. "No, Mom. It's not like that. I didn't think it through—I just . . . I felt safe with him. I didn't even realize how much I've been keeping things from you. I'm sorry. I should have called you."

On the other end, Flower was silent. Finally, she sighed, her tone softer. "I'm glad you're safe. I'm glad someone's protecting you. But I'm still your mother. I need to know these things. Do you understand?"

"I do," Vaughan whispered. "And I'm sorry."

Flower exhaled. "Just promise me you'll be careful. I don't trust this Elias—not yet."

Vaughan glanced at Eli, who now stood with his hand pressed to the crystal, eyes closed. The light around him flickered and flared, casting shadows across the hall. "You don't have to trust him, Mom. I do. And he hasn't given me a reason not to."

Flower hesitated, then finally said, "If you trust him, I'll accept it. But please—don't shut me out again."

"I won't," Vaughan said, though guilt still gnawed at her. They ended the call, and she stood for a moment, clutching the phone.

Eli turned toward her, the glow of the crystal reflecting in his eyes. "You told her," he said quietly.

"Yes," Vaughan said. "She's worried. But she'll come around."

He nodded, stepping closer. "She loves you. That love will matter more than you realize."

Vaughan swallowed hard, feeling the weight of his words. She glanced around the hall again, taking in the shimmer of the crystal orbs, the murmur of unseen forces, the beauty that seemed to breathe. She was enthralled. Whatever secrets this place held, she knew one thing: They were about to change her life forever.

3

FLOWER'S GUILT

Flower sat on the edge of her bed, her thoughts swirling. She couldn't shake the feeling of being the last to know. Her hands trembled as she dialed Sunshine. The phone rang once, twice, before Sunshine answered.

"Flower," Sunshine said softly, as if she already knew why she was calling. "You're upset."

"Yes, I am," Flower said, her voice tight. "Why did she call you first? What does she trust in you that she doesn't in me?"

Sunshine sighed. "It's not about trust, Flower. Vaughan is in a moment of transformation, and sometimes people gravitate toward who feels safest in that instant. You've been her mother, her protector, but my intuition tells me that she also carries the memory of times you weren't emotionally there. That's not your fault, but it's something to acknowledge. She doesn't need you to fix it; she just needs you to stand beside her now."

Flower's chest ached, but Sunshine's words lingered. "What do you mean by that?" Flower asked quietly.

Sunshine hesitated, then said, "I didn't need Vaughan to tell me. I felt it. Intuition doesn't lie, Flower. I've always sensed the moments when you were wrapped in your own ego and spiritual battles—

when you loved her but couldn't reach her. Children pick up on energy, and so do those who are attuned."

Flower exhaled shakily. "So, what do I do?"

"Show her you support her independence, even as an adult," Sunshine said. "Don't cling too tightly. Let her know she can still fall back on you, but also trust her to make her choices. That's how you'll win back her heart."

While Flower absorbed this, Vaughan found Elias waiting by the shimmering hall's doorway. His expression was softer than she'd seen before. "Are you hungry?" he asked.

Vaughan nodded, surprised by the sudden warmth in his tone. Eli led her outside, where the air smelled of something sweet she couldn't name. They followed a winding path to a hidden enclave where lights glowed like stars between trees. It was a small village, rustic yet ethereal, where the people greeted Eli with knowing smiles. These were the people who had shaped him into the Defiance leader he was now.

Over a meal of herbs, bread, and fruits unlike any Vaughan had ever tasted, the villagers spoke of her powers. They explained the secret had to be kept because revealing it too soon would have shattered her understanding of herself. This place only revealed itself to those who were prepared to bear its truth. They told Vaughan of prophecies—how certain energies must align before someone could safely enter. They spoke of doors that would've stayed shut had she come sooner, of dangers that would've devoured her spirit.

Sunshine said, "I have a secret to tell you." She spoke slowly so each revelation sank in. Then she told them the secret was older than any of them, woven into ancient vows that punished those who dared to break them. She described how these oaths were etched not on paper, but in the very fabric of the hall's magic, and how guardians risked losing their minds or lives if they betrayed it.

She explained that the place's magic thrived only in shadows.

Hidden from the unready, it accumulated power like a seed growing underground. If its existence were exposed prematurely, the light would wither it, draining away what made it extraordinary.

As she continued, her voice shivered in the air. Sunshine warned that revealing the truth to someone unprepared invited madness. Minds untrained to carry the weight of this knowledge cracked under its pressure, twisting dreams into nightmares and turning hope into ruin.

She recounted the visits from ghosts she met in childhood. She spoke of her own night—of how a luminous figure appeared beside her bed, whispered vows into her heart, and bound her to silence. Though she was a child, but she understood the gravity. From that night forward, she belonged to this secret.

"Remember the crystal ball I owned with no trinket, Flower?" Sunshine asked.

Flower said, "Yes." It was a fragment of the hall itself, an anchor binding her to this sacred place. When Flower had startled her long ago, Sunshine had hidden it quickly, fearing the oath would punish them both if too much was seen.

The sixth breath was heavy. Sunshine confessed that she had been watched her entire life by unseen forces to ensure she kept her promise. Every choice, every slip of her tongue, every moment of hesitation had been observed. The watchers were relentless, ready to intervene should she falter.

Finally, with the seventh breath, she stressed that timing was everything. Reveal the truth too early, and the fragile threads of destiny would unravel. All their paths would collapse, futures erased before they could bloom. Only when the hall itself signaled readiness could she speak the full truth.

Flower listened, her mind flashing back to her own childhood insecurities, the times she felt abandoned or left out. Hearing that Sunshine knew these things intuitively—and kept them—ignited her frustration.

"You've been keeping secrets from me since we were kids," she said. "Do you know what that did to me? Do you understand how much that makes me feel?"

Sunshine met her gaze calmly. "I knew, Flower. I felt the anger you carried even back then. But the secret wasn't mine to give. The place forbade it, and I obeyed because I knew what disobedience would cost all of us."

Before Flower and the aunt ever stepped into the hall, their journey unfolded like a test of patience and courage. The car ride wound through backroads lined with towering pines, their branches forming a green tunnel that blocked out most of the sky. The hum of the tires over uneven pavement mixed with the sound of wind weaving through leaves.

For long stretches, they rode in silence, Flower glancing at the GPS every so often. Her aunt sat rigid beside her, clutching a worn satchel and avoiding Flower's probing glances.

At times, mist rolled across the road, making the trees blur into ghostly shapes. Flower's chest tightened with every curve. Her thoughts swirled as she thought about Vaughan, Sunshine, and the secrets between her and her sister. The aunt's silence was unnerving; sometimes she would murmur directions under her breath, as if she knew this road too well.

When they finally crossed a stone bridge, the air shifted. The sky deepened into a twilight hue, even though the sun hadn't set. The smell of damp earth and something floral yet unfamiliar filled the car. Flower gripped the steering wheel harder, sensing they were nearing something extraordinary, something she wasn't prepared for.

The drive ended at a clearing shrouded in a glow that seemed to radiate from nowhere and everywhere at once. As Flower parked, she stared at the shimmering path ahead. Her aunt's eyes softened with a knowing glimmer—one that only confirmed Flower's suspicion that she had been here before. They stepped out, the hum of energy in the air almost tangible against their skin.

When they arrived, Flower said, "All these years, you knew, and you never told us?"

The aunt lowered her gaze. "It wasn't my secret to share. The place wouldn't allow it. There are rules—"

Sunshine stepped forward again, reminding Flower of the crystal ball from childhood. "That night, something visited me. It told me not to tell you until the time was right."

Flower's unresolved anxiety rose like a tide. She let Sunshine have it, voicing years of suppressed pain. Vaughan stood by, looking puzzled but agreeing with her mother's anger.

Sunshine, seeming unfazed, said, "The time is now. You were kept from this because you weren't ready. None of us were."

The crystal ball pulsed with calming light, revealing why the truth had waited: To protect them, to prepare them, to make them strong enough to face what was coming.

In that light, Flower's breathing steadied. She lowered her voice. "I don't forgive you yet, Sunshine. But I understand."

Vaughan touched the crystal ball, feeling its energy flow through her. "We can move forward now," she said. "The answers are here, and we'll face them together." The hall glowed brighter as they stood united.

Elias stepped forward quietly. "You've all had a long day," he said, his voice carrying a calm authority. "Come. You need rest before what comes next." He led them through a corridor where crystals embedded in the walls glowed faintly, lighting their path with a soft silver hue.

They entered a wing lined with wooden doors, each carved with intricate symbols that shimmered under the light. Elias opened one door for Vaughan first. Her room was larger than expected, with stone walls that radiated warmth. A bed draped with woven blankets sat against the far wall, and the floor was covered in soft rugs patterned with stars. In the corner, a basin of water reflected the light like liquid glass, and a small table held a single glowing crystal that pulsed gently.

Flower's room was similar but with warmer tones—golden light spilling from a lantern shaped like a blooming flower, and a faint scent of lavender lingering in the air. The aunt's room was darker, its walls adorned with runes that seemed to watch silently. Sunshine's chamber opened into a small balcony where the night sky stretched endlessly, stars close enough to touch.

When they finally lay down, each woman drifted into dreams filled with images of the hall, the crystal ball, and a path winding deeper into the unknown.

As dawn approached, Vaughan awoke first. The air outside was cool, scented with dew and wild herbs. Eli was already waiting in the hallway, leaning against the wall, his eyes distant. "The day begins soon," he said. "What you've seen so far is only the beginning. There are trials ahead—truths you may not be ready to face."

The others emerged, still weary but resolute. Sunshine's gaze was firm, Flower's wary but determined, and the aunt's expression unreadable. Together, they followed Eli back to the main hall, where the crystal ball glowed brighter than ever. The air shimmered with something new—an invitation, or perhaps a warning.

The feeling of the upcoming blood moon weighed heavy in the air. It wasn't just the crimson glow they anticipated—it was the oppressive energy, thick as smoke. Each of them felt it differently: a prickling on the skin, a pounding in the chest, a whisper they could almost hear. But they all knew one thing for certain: They couldn't stop even if they tried.

The house they had taken refuge in felt like a home away from home. It wrapped around them with deceptive warmth, yet the walls seemed to hum with secrets. Every creak of the floorboards and every shift of shadow made the place seem alive. They basked in its comfort, yet none of them understood why they had ended up here— or what had drawn them to this exact spot, under this exact moon.

Vaughan stirred awake long before the others. The air was cold against her skin, the type of cold that crawled up her spine. She rubbed her arms and glanced around. The room was drenched in silver light from the moon, illuminating dust motes that floated like tiny ghosts. Something urged her toward the crystal ball sitting on the table across the room.

Each of her steps felt like it echoed a little too loudly in the stillness. She reached out, fingertips brushing the smooth surface of the orb. It pulsed faintly under her touch—alive.

The crystal ball shimmered, colors swirling inside like storm clouds caught in glass. Then it cleared, revealing something bizarre: a game show, similar to her visions. Bright lights. Flashing numbers. Applause. A distorted host grinning too wide, his teeth unnaturally sharp. Vaughan blinked, unsure if she was dreaming.

The image twisted suddenly, colors bleeding into darkness. The game show vanished. A void consumed the glass, and from that void emerged her—the lady from the beach.

The woman's face was half-hidden by shadows, but her grin was unmistakable, curling upward in something far too wide to be human. Her eyes burned with an unnatural light. She opened her mouth and laughter erupted, not like a human laugh, but a cackle that scraped against Vaughan's eardrums.

Vaughan stumbled back, her hand slipping from the orb. The room seemed to tilt, the floor heaving under her like a ship on rough waters. The air thickened, making it hard to breathe. Her vision blurred, and her knees buckled.

"Vaughan!" Eli's voice cut through the chaos like a blade. He was there in an instant, arms strong and steady as they wrapped around her waist. His grip grounded her, pulling her back from the darkness.

The crystal ball pulsed brighter, as if mocking her. The woman's cackle still rang faintly, echoing.

Flower rushed into the room, her eyes wide, hair disheveled. "Vaughan!" she cried, panic lacing her voice. She knelt beside them, clutching her daughter's hand. A wave of guilt hit her hard, almost knocking the breath from her lungs. She was Vaughan's mother. She was supposed to know—to feel—when something like this was about to happen.

"I should have sensed it," Flower whispered to herself, trembling. "I should have known."

But the truth was, even with her gifts, this place had been clouding her abilities. The house didn't just hide secrets—it devoured them, twisted everything that tried to see too clearly.

Vaughan's breathing was shallow, her eyes fluttering open as Eli steadied her against his chest. "The ball . . . " she said and gasped. "It—it showed her. The woman from the beach. She was laughing. She knows."

"Knows what?" Eli's jaw tightened. His protective instinct had grown stronger with each passing hour. The more this place toyed with them, the more he vowed to fight whatever was lurking in the shadows.

"She knows why we're here," Vaughan whispered, voice shaking. "And she's waiting."

The room fell silent except for the low hum of the orb. Even Flower's sobs ceased as she processed her daughter's words. The blood moon outside was creeping higher, casting a deeper crimson glow through the window. It felt like a countdown had begun.

Eli glanced toward the orb. "We need to destroy that thing."

"No," Flower said sharply, her voice trembling. "It's not just an object. It's a key. You destroy it, and you may destroy our only way out of this."

Eli looked unconvinced, but he didn't argue. Not yet.

The wind outside howled, rattling the windows. The house seemed to shudder, its wooden frame groaning.

Vaughan clutched Eli's shirt, pulling herself upright. Her eyes burned with determination despite the fear. "She's testing us. The woman. She wants to see if we'll break before the moon rises fully."

Flower's breath hitched. "And if we do?"

Vaughan's answer was a whisper, barely audible over the creaking walls. "Then we won't make it to morning."

The rest of the night stretched into a blur of tense silence. Every sound seemed amplified—the ticking of the clock, the moan of the wind, the faint scratches that came from inside the walls. Sleep eluded them, but exhaustion weighed heavily, forcing them to lie down in shifts.

Eli showed them to their rooms, though none of them felt comforted by the idea of being separated. The rooms were simple yet unsettling. Old wooden furniture stood in corners, draped in white sheets that looked like ghosts frozen in place. The wallpaper was peeling, revealing cracks in the plaster beneath.

Vaughan's room was the worst. The mirror above the dresser was cracked, and each shard reflected her face in a distorted, nightmarish way. She avoided looking at it. The bed creaked when she sat, and the mattress sagged as if it had held the weight of something long dead.

Flower's room was colder, the windows streaked with condensation from the fog outside. The air smelled faintly of mildew and something metallic—like blood. She shivered, wrapping a blanket around her shoulders.

Eli's room felt suffocating. The ceiling sloped low, and the corners of the room seemed to stretch farther than they should, like the geometry was wrong. He kept the door open, just in case.

As they each settled in, the house grew eerily quiet. The crystal ball glowed faintly in the other room, unattended but not dormant.

At precisely midnight, the blood moon reached its peak. Its light poured through the windows, staining everything crimson. Vaughan stirred in her bed, eyes snapping open. She heard it again—the woman's unmistakable cackle.

A shadow slipped across her wall, long and distorted.

Vaughan sat up and glanced at the door. It was still closed. Yet the shadow moved again, crawling along the wall like something alive.

"Eli . . . " she whispered, but no sound came out.

The doorknob turned slowly.

The silence that followed was unbearable. Each breath they took seemed to echo through the empty halls, bouncing back at them like whispers from unseen mouths. For a brief moment, none of them spoke. They were too exhausted, too shaken.

Eli broke the silence first. "We need to leave this place." His voice was hoarse, raw from shouting.

Flower stared at the faintly pulsing shard on the floor. "We can't—not yet. Not until we know what she's tied to. That shard means she's still anchored here."

Although upheaval was occurring, Flower was listening to her spirit more than her ego.

Vaughan hugged her knees to her chest, rocking slightly. "She said we belonged to her. What did she mean?"

No one answered. A wind blew through the room, though the windows were shut. It smelled of rot and damp earth, as if something old and buried had just been unearthed.

Eli's jaw clenched. "We destroy that shard now."

Flower reached out quickly. "No! If you destroy it the wrong way, she'll spread. That piece holds her essence. We need to contain it."

The shard pulsed brighter, and an almost imperceptible laugh drifted through the air.

Vaughan shivered. "She's listening to us."

Flower nodded grimly. "She always is."

They gathered the shard carefully, wrapping it in an old cloth Flower found in the room. Even through the fabric, it radiated a cold energy that numbed their fingers.

Eli took it and shoved it into his jacket pocket. "Then we keep it close. And when the time's right, we destroy it for good."

The house seemed to sigh at their decision, its wooden frame settling. But the quiet wasn't comforting—it was watchful.

They needed rest, but none of them dared sleep alone. They dragged blankets into the main hall, forming a makeshift camp in the center of the room where they could see each other.

The fire in the old stone fireplace burned low, casting long shadows that danced across the walls. Each flicker seemed to shape itself into faces, distorted and screaming. Vaughan tried not to look too long.

Time stretched unnaturally. The sound of the clock ticking was maddening, louder than it had any right to be.

At some point, Eli dozed off, his hand still gripping the chair leg. Flower sat against the wall, her eyes half-closed but alert, lips moving silently in protective prayers.

Vaughan was the only one fully awake when she heard it—a scratching sound. Faint, deliberate. Not from outside. From inside the walls.

Her heart leaped into her throat. She nudged Flower, who opened her eyes immediately. The scratching grew louder, closer.

Then came the voice. Soft at first, like a child whispering secrets:

"Vaughan . . . come to me . . . "

The hairs on Vaughan's arms stood on end. It wasn't the woman—it was someone else. Someone younger, pleading.

She stood slowly, ignoring Flower's protest, and followed the sound toward the far wall. Her hand touched the peeling wallpaper, and the scratching stopped abruptly.

A faint outline appeared—small handprints pressing from the inside.

Vaughan stumbled back. The handprints smeared down the wall as if something was sliding lower, weaker.

The voice whimpered. "Help me . . . "

Eli jolted awake and rushed to her side. "What is that?"

Flower's face went pale. "There's more than one spirit here. She's not alone."

The handprints faded, leaving behind a streak of black residue. The smell of decay filled the room.

Flower whispered, "This house has been feeding her victims to itself for years."

A loud bang shook the ceiling. Dust rained down. The walls moaned, vibrating with an unnatural force.

Eli tightened his grip on the shard in his pocket. "We need to get out—*now*."

But when they rushed to the front door, it wouldn't budge. The knob turned freely, but the door stayed shut, as if it were fused to the frame.

They tried the windows. Each one was sealed, glass cold to the touch, unyielding like stone.

The house was trapping them.

A laugh echoed, not from the shard, but from the walls. Low at first, then louder, until it felt like the entire building was cackling.

Flower clutched her chest, gasping. "She's merging with the house. Every piece of it is her."

The floorboards beneath their feet warped, twisting into jagged shapes. A crack split down the middle of the room, glowing faintly red as if the house itself was bleeding.

Vaughan screamed as a hand shot up from the crack—gray, clawed, grasping. It tried to grab her ankle, but Eli yanked her back just in time.

More hands emerged, clawing at the air. The smell of sulfur filled the room.

They retreated to the staircase, climbing quickly as the floor below writhed like a pit of serpents. The house groaned in fury, the walls closing in around them.

Upstairs, they slammed the door to the nearest room, barricading it with an old dresser. Their breaths came in ragged gasps.

For a moment, everything was still. Too still.

Then came the knock. Soft. Slow. Coming from the other side of the door.

No one moved.

The knock came again, louder. Then a voice, sweet and coaxing: "Let me in . . . "

Vaughan pressed her back to the wall, tears streaking her face. "It's her. She's pretending."

The knocking turned into pounding, shaking the door. The voice twisted into a guttural scream.

Eli held his weapon tight, ready to fight, but Flower knew brute force wouldn't save them this time.

She grabbed Vaughan's hands. "Listen to me. You are stronger than her. She wants fear—don't give it to her."

The door cracked. Splinters flew.

The shard in Eli's pocket pulsed violently, almost burning. He pulled it out, and as soon as it hit the open air, the pounding stopped.

The voice hissed, venomous. "You'll regret that."

The shard glowed brighter, almost painfully. Flower's eyes widened. "She's trying to pull herself back through it."

Eli glared at it, his knuckles white. "Then we end this—tonight."

Vaughan took a deep breath, wiping her tears. "Tell us what to do."

Flower's voice was steady now. "There's an altar in the attic. That's where the final seal is. We take the shard there, finish the ritual—and burn this place to the ground."

They exchanged a glance. No turning back now.

With the shard pulsing like a heartbeat in Eli's hand, they crept toward the attic stairs. Each step creaked, the sound magnified in the suffocating silence.

As they climbed, the house seemed to resist, the steps stretching, twisting. The air grew heavy, hard to breathe.

At the top, a single wooden door awaited, etched with strange symbols that glowed faintly in the moonlight streaming through a cracked window.

Eli pushed it open, and the attic revealed itself: an altar covered in dried blood, surrounded by candles that lit themselves as they entered.

The woman's laughter filled the space, louder than ever. "Welcome to my home."

The candles flared, shadows twisting into monstrous shapes. The shard burned in Eli's hand, screaming with energy.

Vaughan stepped forward, heart pounding. "Do it. End her."

Flower chanted again, louder than before. The air vibrated with power, the symbols on the walls glowing brighter.

Eli slammed the shard onto the altar, driving it into the center with all his strength.

The room exploded with light. The woman screamed, a sound so shrill it rattled their bones. Flames erupted, consuming the altar, the walls, everything.

They ran down the stairs, through the twisting halls, until they burst through the front door—which finally gave way, spitting them out into the night.

The house burned behind them, roaring with fury, its windows like eyes glaring as it collapsed.

They packed up their stuff and rode in the cold night air, watching some of it burn until nothing was left but ash.

When the last ember died, Vaughan felt a cold hand brush hers. She turned—no one was there.

A faint voice whispered in her ear: "This isn't over."

The fire that devoured the house burned for hours, reducing it to blackened rubble under the pale light of the returning moon. The last embers collapse inward. Every crackle sounded like a whisper, every plume of smoke like a ghost escaping into the night sky.

None of them needed to speak—they had survived something no words could ever explain to the outside world.

When dawn finally broke, the first rays of sunlight felt unreal. Warm, golden light spread across their faces, and for the first time in what felt like centuries, they weren't shrouded in crimson.

Eli stretched his aching arms, his eyes scanning the tree line as if expecting something to emerge. His protective stance never softened. Even in daylight, he didn't trust that they were safe.

Flower brushed soot off her clothes, her expression set in its usual mix of sternness and worry. "We need to leave this place," she said, her voice trembling beneath its edge. "Now."

Vaughan nodded weakly. Her body felt like it weighed a hundred pounds. "We'll pack what we can. Then we're gone."

The magical place that had once felt like a haven—warm fires, enchanted rooms, quiet woods—was now cold and hollow. Whatever forces had protected them there had withdrawn during the blood moon, leaving them exposed to the woman's wrath.

As they entered the remnants of the house to salvage their

belongings, Vaughan felt eyes on her again. Not hostile—just . . . watching. The energy was softer, almost regretful. She thought of the other presences in the house, the voices trapped in the walls, the small hands that had cried for help.

"Where are they?" she murmured.

"Who?" Eli asked.

"The protectors. The ones who should've kept her away. This place was supposed to have magic—it was supposed to shield us."

Flower overheard, shaking her head. "They're gone, Vaughan. Probably left long before we came. Or maybe they were killed by her."

The thought made Vaughan shiver. The house hadn't just been a prison—it had been a battlefield, one they had unknowingly stepped into.

They gathered their things quickly. Flower packed with precision, muttering under her breath like each item she folded was a ritual of its own. Eli threw essentials into his bag, never letting the shard out of his sight. Vaughan moved slower, touching objects as if saying goodbye.

By midday, they were ready to leave. The charred ruin of the house sat behind them like a tombstone. None of them looked back as they walked down the dirt road toward the cars parked at the edge of the forest.

Flower glanced at Vaughan, her eyes narrowing slightly when she noticed Eli walking close to her. "What are your plans?" she asked sharply.

"I'm going home," Vaughan said. The words felt strange. Home sounded like a dream after what they'd endured.

"I'm coming with you," Eli said firmly, no hesitation in his tone.

Flower stopped walking. "No. You're not."

Vaughan turned, startled. "Mom—"

"I don't trust him." Flower crossed her arms, her tone hard. "Every time he's around, something happens. Bad omens. He's bad news."

Eli's jaw tightened. "I saved her life. More than once. You really think I'd hurt her?"

"I think trouble follows you," Flower snapped.

The tension crackled between them like the energy in the house had. Vaughan stepped between them. "Enough! Both of you. We just survived a storm—I'm not doing this here."

Flower's glare softened slightly, but her pride still burned in her eyes. "You'll regret letting him stay."

Eli looked at Vaughan. "It's your call."

Vaughan took a breath. "He stays. But in the guest room."

Flower scoffed but said nothing more. She knew arguing would only push her daughter further away.

They reached the cars in silence. Flower got into hers without a word, driving off toward her own home. Eli and Vaughan shared a long glance before climbing into her car.

The ride was quiet, the world outside unnaturally calm. Sunlight streamed through the windshield, warm and golden, as if nothing had ever happened. It was almost enough to convince them they were safe.

But as they drove away, Vaughan caught sight of something in the rearview mirror—a figure standing in the ash of the burned house, watching them go.

When she blinked, it was gone.

The road stretched endlessly, framed by trees whose branches bent as if leaning toward the car, watching. The further they got from the burned ruins, the more the world seemed to return to normal. But she knew—normal was an illusion.

Eli sat silently in the passenger seat, his hand resting over the pocket where he still kept the wrapped shard. Even now, it throbbed faintly. Every few minutes, he'd glance at it.

Vaughan noticed. "Does it still . . . glow?" she asked hesitantly.

"Sometimes," he said. "It's not done with us."

When they finally reached her house, relief washed over her. The sight of the familiar porch, the flower pots she had left behind, and the wind chimes tinkling softly in the breeze felt almost like stepping into a dream she'd forgotten she had.

Eli carried in the bags while Vaughan unlocked the door. The house smelled like home—lavender from the candles, the faint scent of wood polish.

Flower's car was already parked outside her own house several blocks away. She had driven off quickly after their argument, but Vaughan knew her mother's pride meant she wouldn't apologize anytime soon.

Inside, Eli placed the bags down, glancing around. "You have a nice place," he said quietly, almost like he didn't want to disturb the peace here.

Vaughan gave a weak smile. "Thanks. You'll stay in the guest room. It's down the hall."

She showed him to the room. It was simple but cozy—soft bedding, a dresser, and a small window that overlooked the backyard. She had prepared it long ago for visitors, never expecting it to be used for someone like him.

Eli set his bag down and nodded. "This will work."

That night, they tried to settle in. Vaughan showered, letting the hot water wash away the soot and tension. She slipped into bed, but sleep didn't come easy. Each time she closed her eyes, she saw flashes of the clawed hands, the flames devouring the house.

Across the hall, Eli lay awake too, staring at the ceiling. He kept the shard in his bag beside the bed, close enough to grab if something happened. It emitted a faint, cold glow that cast eerie shadows on the walls.

Meanwhile, Flower sat in her own home, staring at the walls like they were whispering secrets she couldn't quite hear. Why hadn't she sensed this danger sooner? Why hadn't she protected Vaughan better? The thought of Eli being in her daughter's house only made the unease worse.

"He's trouble," she muttered to herself, pacing. "Something about him attracts darkness."

Over the next few days, life seemed to settle. Vaughan cooked simple meals. She and Eli cleaned the soot off what few belongings they had salvaged. Flower visited once, her disapproval radiating from every movement, but she stayed only long enough to bring herbs and protections she claimed would ward off any lingering spirits.

Eli thanked her, though the look they exchanged was cold. Flower's distrust ran deep, and Eli's patience for her accusations was thin.

Vaughan returned to work, though her coworkers noticed she was quieter, more withdrawn. Eli stayed at her house, helping with repairs and errands. The shard remained locked in a small wooden box in the guest room, wrapped in layers of cloth.

At night, however, lights flickered. Doors creaked open on their own. The wind outside carried whispers that weren't quite the wind.

One morning, Vaughan found the box with the shard slightly open, though she swore she had locked it. Eli denied touching it, and the argument that followed was tense with unspoken fear.

Flower called later that day, her voice sharp. "I told you something bad would happen. Get rid of him before it's too late."

"Mom, stop," Vaughan snapped. "You're blaming him for things we can't explain. You're making this worse."

Flower hissed through the phone, "Mark my words, Vaughan. He's the reason the bad omens are following you."

When she hung up, Vaughan's hands shook. She didn't want to admit it, but part of her wondered if Flower was right.

That evening, as the sun dipped below the horizon, the house grew unnaturally cold. Eli stood by the window, scanning the darkening street. "She's not gone," he said quietly.

Vaughan turned to him, startled. "Who?"

"The woman. I can feel her. She's out there, waiting."

Before Vaughan could respond, the wind chimes outside rattled violently, though there was no wind. A shadow darted across the yard, too fast to be human. Eli grabbed his weapon instinctively.

When they opened the door, the yard was empty. Silent.

But the feeling of being watched was overwhelming.

Later that night, Vaughan dreamed of the burned house. She stood among the ashes, and the woman's voice whispered, "You can burn my cage, but you can't burn me."

She woke up screaming. Eli rushed into the room, gripping her shoulders. "It's just a dream," he said, but his eyes betrayed his own fear.

Across town, Flower woke at the same time, sitting upright in bed. She swore she had heard Vaughan's scream in her mind.

The next morning, Flower drove to Vaughan's house unannounced. When Eli opened the door, she pushed past him, glaring. "I'm staying here for a few days."

Vaughan blinked, surprised. "Why?"

"To protect you," Flower said firmly. "Someone has to, since he can't."

Eli muttered under his breath, "Here we go again."

The two clashed constantly over the following days. Flower accused Eli of being a magnet for evil, while Eli argued she was letting her pride blind her to what was really happening. Vaughan was caught in the middle, exhaustion carving deep lines into her face.

Despite their conflict, they all felt the same thing: The curse wasn't done with them.

The protectors who were supposed to guard the magical place were nowhere to be found. The absence was glaring like a hole in the world. Vaughan asked herself repeatedly: Where were they when the house turned on them? Why hadn't they intervened?

One night, as they sat in the dim living room, Eli said, "Maybe they're dead. Or worse—maybe they're trapped like the other spirits we heard."

Flower crossed her arms, scoffing. "Convenient excuse."

But deep down, she feared he was right.

In the nights that followed, they ate dinner together, laughed once or twice, even watched the sunset from the porch. For a while, it felt like the nightmare had passed.

But dead birds appeared in the yard. Vaughan's mirrors cracked on their own. The shard glowed brighter with each passing night.

Life was only calm because the storm hadn't reached them yet. And they weren't prepared for what was coming.

Then another sign came at dawn. Vaughan was making tea when she noticed the steam from the kettle rise unnaturally, twisting into the shape of a face before dissolving. The eyes that formed in the vapor burned into her mind long after the steam disappeared.

When she told Eli, he only nodded grimly. "She's testing boundaries."

Flower overheard and scoffed. "Or maybe the boundaries are breaking because of him." She pointed accusingly at Eli, whose jaw clenched.

"That's enough," Vaughan snapped. "We're all in this together— whether you like it or not."

The argument was cut short when the lights flickered, buzzing as if overloaded. One by one, they went out, plunging the house into semi-darkness despite the morning sun streaming through the windows.

The air turned icy cold. Their breath became visible.

A whisper filled the room, soft but chilling: "You can't hide from me."

The sound came from everywhere at once, echoing off the walls. Flower clutched the pendant around her neck, muttering a protection chant under her breath. Eli grabbed the shard box, which glowed faintly through its wrappings.

Every cabinet door in the kitchen slammed open at once, plates shattering to the floor. The violent clatter made Vaughan scream.

"She's in the house," Eli growled, stepping in front of Vaughan protectively.

Flower raised her voice, shouting her own chant over the chaos. The room vibrated with energy, the shards of glass trembling on the floor.

The three of them stood frozen, hearts pounding. Vaughan's hands shook as she gripped the edge of the counter. "She's not bound to the house anymore. She's bound to us."

Eli nodded grimly. "And she's growing stronger."

That night, Vaughan barely slept. When she finally drifted off, she dreamed she was walking through a field of ash. The woman from the beach stood at the far end, smiling with her jagged grin. "You thought you escaped me?" she whispered. "I'm everywhere you go."

When Vaughan woke, there were ash footprints on her bedroom floor—leading to her bed.

The next day, a crow flew straight into the window and broke its neck. The clocks stopped ticking at exactly 3:33 a.m. The water from the taps ran black for several seconds before clearing.

Flower's kept sprinkling salt around the house and burning sage until the air was thick with smoke. She said, "Eli, you're the reason she's still here. She wants you as much as she wants my daughter."

Eli glared. "Maybe she wants both of us, but I'm the only one willing to fight her."

Vaughan slammed her hands on the table. "Enough! We have to stop tearing each other apart—that's what she wants."

Despite Vaughan's plea, the tension remained. Flower was also startled at Vaughan's response. They hadn't had many disagreements, and Vaughan never yelled. Something about the energy was extracting a true, yet angry nature from everyone. Flower slept with one eye open, clutching her pendant like a weapon. Eli kept the shard box under his pillow, convinced the woman was trying to reclaim it.

The protectors' absence gnawed at Vaughan. They were supposed to be there to shield this realm, to keep the dark forces from leaking into the human world. If they were gone, it meant something much worse was at play.

One evening, while Vaughan was alone in the living room, the temperature dropped again. She could see her breath as she looked around nervously.

The TV flickered on by itself. Static filled the screen, then shifted to the image of the burned house. Vaughan's heart raced. The screen zoomed into the ashes, and out of the blackened ruin, the woman's hand reached toward the camera.

The TV exploded, sparks flying. Vaughan fell back with a scream as the smell of burned plastic filled the room.

Eli came running, grabbing her arm. "Are you okay?"

"She's coming through everything now." Vaughan gasped. "Walls, mirrors, even the TV. There's nowhere safe."

The following days blurred into a nightmare cycle of terror. Strange accidents happened constantly: knives fell from countertops on their own, doors slammed with enough force to crack frames, and once, Flower narrowly avoided being crushed when a shelf collapsed.

Flower grew more hostile toward Eli. "You need to leave," she demanded one night. "You're making this worse."

"I'm not leaving her," Eli said coldly. "If you want to go, go."

Flower's eyes narrowed. "You think you can protect her? You can't even protect yourself."

But she didn't leave. Deep down, she knew that whatever darkness hunted them, it was too strong to face alone.

For a few days, the activity stopped, as if the entity had retreated. They ate dinner in peace, slept without nightmares, even laughed at small things.

Vaughan hoped maybe it was over.

But on the fourth night, a storm rolled in. The wind howled, rain pounded the windows, and thunder shook the house. In the midst of the storm, Vaughan heard it: the cackle.

She ran to Eli's room, and together they watched as the shard's box glowed brighter than ever. It pulsed violently, rattling on the dresser.

Flower burst in, her face pale. "She's coming through the shard. We have to do something—now."

The lights went out, plunging them into darkness. Only the glow of the shard illuminated the room, casting eerie shadows on their faces.

The woman's voice filled the house, booming and distorted: "You thought you burned me away. You only set me free."

The walls shook. The floors buckled. A mirror shattered, and from the shards, her shadow emerged, then crawled into the room.

Vaughan clutched Eli's arm. Flower screamed words of power, her voice rising above the storm.

But this time, the woman was stronger than chants. She stepped fully into the room, her form flickering between shadow and flesh. Her grin stretched unnaturally wide.

"You're mine now," she hissed.

Eli stepped forward, gripping the shard with bare hands despite its burning heat. "Not tonight."

The woman lunged. Eli's hands smoked as the shard burned into his skin, but he didn't let go.

Her form elongated unnaturally, claws slicing through the air where he stood moments before. He dodged, slamming the shard against the floor. The impact sent a shockwave through the room, making the walls vibrate like an earthquake.

The woman shrieked, her voice splitting the air. The sound was so piercing Vaughan had to cover her ears, collapsing to her knees. Flower chanted louder, forcing her voice to rise above the chaos, invoking names older than the earth itself.

Darkness rippled around her, her form flickering like a dying flame. But she wasn't weakening—she was adapting. With a guttural roar, she spread her arms wide, and every light source in the house exploded in a shower of sparks.

Now the only glow came from her and the shard, two forces colliding in the dim room.

"You can't stop me," she said, her voice splitting into multiple tones. "The protectors abandoned this world long ago. I'm free because they're gone."

Vaughan's heart pounded. "Why us? Why are you after us?"

The woman turned her gaze to her, eyes burning. "Because you carry what they lost. You are the link. You are the key."

Before Vaughan could ask what that meant, the ceiling above them cracked violently. A blinding light spilled through, and figures descended, cloaked in shimmering mist. Their forms were indistinct, but their presence was undeniable.

"The protectors." Flower gasped, shielding her eyes.

The woman screamed in fury, twisting into a shadow to escape their light, but they surrounded her, forming a circle. Their voices merged into a single resonant chant, ancient and commanding.

Vaughan clutched Eli's arm, both of them frozen. The protectors' power filled the room, pressing against every surface like a tidal wave.

The woman thrashed, shrieking curses in an ancient language. Her claws tore through the walls, but the protectors held firm. Their light burned her shadowy form, forcing her to shrink.

Eli, still holding the shard, felt its energy surge through him. His veins burned like fire, but he understood what he needed to do. "Vaughan—take it. You're the link she's after. You're the one who can end this."

Terrified, Vaughan hesitated, but Eli thrust the shard into her hands. The moment she touched it, a jolt of power shot through her, nearly knocking her off her feet. The protectors' chanting grew louder.

The woman lunged at Vaughan one last time, her form a blur of shadow and teeth. Vaughan raised the shard high, screaming, and drove it into the ground.

Light exploded outward, blinding and pure. The woman's scream shattered the air, echoing as her form disintegrated into black ash that was sucked into the shard.

The protectors stood still for a moment, their glowing forms watching Vaughan. One stepped forward, speaking in a voice like wind through the trees. "You have done what we could not. But know this—the darkness is never truly gone. It waits."

Vaughan tried to speak, but her voice caught in her throat.

The protector extended a hand toward her, touching her forehead lightly. A surge of warmth spread through her, and she heard a whisper in her mind: "You are one of us now. Whether you choose it or not."

Then, as quickly as they came, the protectors vanished, leaving only the faint scent of ozone and the echo of their voices.

Eli collapsed against the wall, breathing heavily. "It's over . . . right?"

Flower looked at Vaughan. "I don't think it's over. I think this was only the beginning."

The house felt different now, no longer oppressive, but not entirely safe either. The air was still charged with something they couldn't name.

Vaughan held the shard, now dim and cold. Its power had quieted, but she felt it still pulsing faintly in her hand like a heartbeat.

Over the next hours, they sat together in silence, too drained to speak. The storm outside had passed, leaving the sky eerily clear.

When dawn broke, they made a decision. Flower would return to her home, needing space to process what had happened. She still didn't trust Eli, but she no longer had the energy to argue.

Vaughan and Eli packed their things. They couldn't stay in the house where the woman had walked among them. Every corner whispered of her presence.

Before Flower left, she pulled Vaughan aside. "You may think you're safe now, but keep your eyes open. Darkness follows those who've touched it."

Vaughan nodded, hugging her mother tightly. "I'll be careful."

4

———

A NEW SCENERY

Eli drove them to a new place, one Vaughan had rented far from the city. It was a small cottage near the woods, quiet and unassuming. For a while, it felt like a sanctuary.

They set up the guest room for Eli, keeping the shard locked in a box beneath the floorboards. Vaughan didn't dare destroy it—something told her it wasn't ready to be destroyed yet.

Days passed peacefully. They laughed again, cooked meals, watched the sun set. Life felt almost normal, and they let themselves believe maybe the nightmare was truly over.

But then the bad omens returned.

It started small—dead insects gathered at the windowsills, the mirrors fogging without reason. Then came the dreams, darker and more vivid than before. Vaughan woke nightly with the taste of ash in her mouth.

Eli noticed shadows moving in the corners of rooms when there was nothing to cast them. The shard began to glow faintly again.

Flower called, her voice shaking. "Have you felt it? It's not over. Something worse is coming."

That night, Vaughan stood outside the cottage, staring into the woods. The trees swayed though there was no wind. Between the trunks, she saw a pair of glowing eyes staring back at her.

The woman's voice whispered on the breeze, soft but clear: "You think you're safe? You've only opened the door wider."

Vaughan's breath hitched. She turned to run inside, but when she glanced back, the eyes were gone.

She leaned against the door, trembling. The protectors had saved them once, but they hadn't destroyed the evil—only delayed it.

Inside, Eli stood waiting, weapon in hand. "What did you see?"

Vaughan swallowed hard. "It's starting again."

And they both knew—the next battle would be worse than the last.

The following morning was eerily quiet. The sunlight that filtered through the cottage windows seemed dimmer, as though something was feeding on it. Vaughan sat at the kitchen table, hands wrapped around her mug, staring blankly at the steam rising from her tea.

Eli watched her from across the room. "You didn't sleep again."

"No," she said. "Every time I close my eyes, I see her. Or . . . something worse. Something bigger than her."

Eli's brow furrowed. "Bigger?"

Vaughan nodded slowly. "In my dreams, she's kneeling to something—something cloaked in shadows so dense they swallowed the light. It was like . . . she was only a servant."

Eli rubbed his face, exhaling sharply. "So she's not the endgame. She's a messenger."

Before Vaughan could respond, the phone rang. It was Flower. Her voice was frantic. "Vaughan, you need to leave that house—now. I had a vision last night. Something's coming for you."

Vaughan's grip on the phone tightened. "What did you see?"

"Smoke," Flower whispered. "And hands—hundreds of them, reaching for you. Eli was there too, but he . . . he was bleeding. And something took you both."

The line crackled, and for a moment Vaughan thought she heard a faint whisper on the other end. Then the call dropped.

Eli grabbed the phone. "What did she say?"

Vaughan's lips trembled. "She saw something coming. And it's not her—it's something worse."

They spent the day reinforcing the cottage—locking windows, sprinkling salt at thresholds, burning herbs Flower had left behind. But deep down, they knew none of it would hold back what was hunting them.

That night, as they tried to rest, the woods surrounding the cottage came alive. The sound of footsteps echoed outside, multiple sets, circling the house.

Eli grabbed his weapon and stood by the window, peering into the darkness. The shapes outside were barely visible, but their glowing eyes pierced the night.

"They're watching us," he growled.

Vaughan stayed back, clutching the shard box. It vibrated violently, as though whatever was outside was trying to draw it out.

The front door rattled, the handle turning on its own. Eli held it shut with all his strength, his muscles straining.

The whispers came next, soft and overlapping, speaking in a language neither of them understood. The sound wormed into Vaughan's head, dizzying her.

"Stay with me!" Eli shouted, snapping her out of it.

The voices stopped abruptly, leaving the night silent again. But the silence was worse than the noise—it meant they were waiting.

In the morning, they found the yard covered in ash footprints. Vaughan's stomach churned at the sight.

When Flower arrived later that day, she was pale, her hands trembling. "You're not fighting just one entity anymore. They're gathering. She's only the first."

Eli frowned. "Who's 'they?'"

"The ones she serves," Flower said darkly. "The real darkness. The light defenders told me—they're breaking through."

Vaughan's heart sank. "The light defenders spoke to you?"

Flower nodded. "Briefly. They said you've been marked as a vessel. If they take you, it's over—not just for us, but for a lot more."

Eli clenched his fists. "Then we don't let them take her. Ever."

That night, the attacks resumed, more violent. Objects hurled across rooms, windows cracked despite being reinforced, and the lights burst into flames without warning.

Eli fought to hold the barrier while Flower chanted desperately, her voice hoarse. Vaughan stood at the center, clutching the shard, feeling its power swell.

The woman's voice returned, echoing through the house. "You can't stop the ones I serve. I was only the beginning."

The walls bled black liquid that dripped down like tar. The smell was nauseating. Vaughan screamed as the floor beneath her feet burned with glowing symbols, searing into the wood.

The light defenders appeared again, but this time, their forms were dimmer, weaker, their light flickering. One of them spoke in a strained voice: "We cannot hold them back much longer. You must find the source."

"What source?" Vaughan cried.

"The origin of the curse," the protector said, their voice fading. "It lies where the veil is thinnest—where she was born."

Then they vanished, leaving only their warning.

Eli turned to Vaughan, gripping her shoulders. "We need to find where this all started. Whatever she came from—we end it there."

Flower shook her head. "You'll be walking straight into their nest."

"We don't have a choice," Vaughan whispered. "If we don't, they'll come for everyone."

But before they could leave, the doors slammed shut. Windows sealed themselves. The walls bulged inward as if the house was breathing.

The whispers rose again, louder, screaming in unison: "*Stay*."

Eli grabbed Vaughan's hand. "Run!"

They crashed through the back door just as the house erupted in flames behind them. The night sky glowed red, smoke rising into the stars.

From the trees, dozens of glowing eyes watched as they fled. The whispers followed: "You can't run from what's already inside you."

The night after the townhouse burned, they drove in silence. Vaughan sat in the backseat, her heart aching as she watched the faint glow of the fire fade in the distance. That townhouse had been her sanctuary—warm, alive with memories she thought were untouchable. Now it was ash.

She was grateful they had managed to grab the essentials—the photo albums she couldn't replace and her journals filled with years of thoughts. Eli had insisted they take what mattered, working fast while the house itself seemed to push them out. They'd left behind furniture, dishes, things that could be bought again. But the soul of the place—its energy—was gone forever.

Vaughan's chest tightened. It wasn't just a home that had burned. It felt like a part of her had burned with it.

She clenched the shard in her hands, the cold pulse of it vibrating faintly against her skin. Even in its silence, it reminded her that their fight wasn't over. She held it tightly, as though it were the only thing keeping her anchored to reality.

The road ahead stretched endlessly, a black ribbon winding through dense forests and empty highways. The trees seemed to lean closer to the car as they passed, their branches reaching into the darkness. The smell of smoke clung to them, creeping into their hair and skin.

Eli drove without speaking. His silence wasn't cold; it was protective, the kind of silence that said he was listening to everything—the road, the night, the unseen things moving just beyond the headlights.

Flower sat in the passenger seat, her eyes closed, but Vaughan knew she wasn't sleeping. Her mother's breathing was shallow, her fingers twitching as if counting silent prayers.

In the backseat, Vaughan rested her forehead against the cold glass of the window. The reflection that stared back at her looked different—tired, hardened, yet burning with something she couldn't name.

The moon hung low in the sky, half-hidden behind a veil of clouds, its pale light streaking the highway. Every few miles, Vaughan swore she saw shapes in the mist, flickering shadows that vanished when she blinked.

She clung to the shard. She didn't know why she had bought the second townhouse years ago. At the time, it felt unnecessary, even foolish. But something inside her—some quiet voice she had learned to trust—told her to do it.

Now, that intuition felt like the only thing keeping them one step ahead of whatever darkness still lurked behind them.

She took a shaky breath, the cold glass against her skin grounding her. "We'll make it," she whispered, not sure if she was talking to Eli, Flower, or herself.

Neither of them responded, but she felt Eli's eyes glance at her in the rearview mirror for just a moment, as if to say, *You're right. We will.*

Still, Vaughan felt like something was following them—something the fire hadn't destroyed. The road stretched on, and she wondered if the darkness was simply waiting for the right moment to strike again.

Every tree they passed seemed to twist unnaturally, the branches reaching for the car like claws. Eli gripped the steering wheel harder with each mile, his jaw tense. Flower rode in the passenger seat, arms crossed, eyes closed as she muttered protective prayers under her breath.

After hours, they stopped at a small, rundown motel on the outskirts of a forgotten town. The air smelled stale, the neon sign outside buzzing faintly. Inside, the rooms were dingy, but they had no choice. They needed rest.

Eli checked the locks twice before setting down his bag. "We keep watches tonight. No one sleeps alone."

Flower rolled her eyes. "You think the locks matter? If they want in, they'll get in."

Vaughan sat on the bed, still holding the shard. It pulsed faintly in her hands, and for the first time, she noticed something strange: It glowed brighter when her fear spiked. When she calmed her breathing, the glow dimmed.

She didn't tell the others. Not yet.

That night, while Eli kept first watch, Vaughan dreamed again. But this time, it wasn't the woman—it was something bigger, deeper. Shadows swirled around her, whispering in hundreds of voices, telling her she was theirs.

In the center of the darkness stood a figure cloaked in black smoke. Its face was obscured, but its presence was suffocating. "You create what you fear," it hissed. "Fear me, and I grow."

She woke with a start, gasping. The shard on the nightstand was glowing fiercely.

Eli rushed to her side. "Another dream?"

Vaughan nodded, trembling. "It said . . . it said I create what I fear."

Flower stirred, her eyes narrowing. "What does that mean?"

Vaughan hesitated. "I think we're feeding it. Every time we're afraid, it gets stronger."

Flower frowned. "That doesn't make sense."

"Doesn't it?" Eli said quietly. "Think about it. Every attack—it got worse when we panicked. When we fought back with clarity, it weakened."

Flower bit her lip but said nothing more.

They left at dawn, following the coordinates Flower had pieced together from her visions. The path took them deeper into the mountains, where mist clung to the trees and the air grew heavier with every step.

Hours passed before they reached a clearing. The ground was cracked, and strange symbols were etched into the stones. The air here was electric, alive. Vaughan knew instantly—this was the origin.

The shard pulsed violently, almost as if it wanted to leap out of her hand.

Eli stepped forward cautiously. "This is it."

The sky darkened without warning. Wind whipped through the clearing, carrying whispers that grew louder with every passing second.

Flower shouted above the roar. "They know we're here!"

The ground split open, and from the fissures rose the woman, her form massive now, her grin wider than ever. Behind her, the cloaked figure towered, its presence overwhelming.

"You came to me," it hissed. "You brought exactly what I needed."

The woman lunged, but Vaughan didn't move. Something inside her shifted. She remembered the dream. The words.

You create what you fear.

The protectors appeared, faint and flickering, unable to fully manifest. Their voices overlapped: "Do not feed it."

Eli raised his weapon, ready to attack, but Vaughan grabbed his arm. "No. That's what it wants."

The woman hissed, twisting toward her. "Fight me. Fear me. Make me strong."

Vaughan closed her eyes, forcing her breathing to slow. She focused on something else—not the fear, not the darkness—something stronger. The warmth of the sun. The sound of laughter. The feeling of home.

The voices screamed. The ground shook. The woman shrieked in rage.

Flower stared at her daughter, realization dawning on her face. "She's not fighting. She's . . . unmaking them."

The cloaked figure roared, its form expanding, trying to drown her out with darkness. But the more Vaughan focused on peace, the more it faded.

"You don't control me," Vaughan said, her voice steady. "You only exist because I let you."

The shard in her hand began to disintegrate into light, scattering into the air. The woman's form cracked like glass, her laughter turning into screams.

The cloaked figure howled, its body unraveling into smoke. "You can't destroy what you are!"

Vaughan opened her eyes, glowing with a strange light. "I'm not you. I'm stronger."

With one final surge of will, she released the last of her fear. The clearing erupted in blinding white light.

When the light faded, the figures were gone. The ground was whole again. The sky was clear. The protectors stood, no longer flickering, their forms solid and radiant.

One stepped forward. "You have passed the test. You have proven that strength is not in fighting the darkness, but in refusing to create it."

Vaughan collapsed into Eli's arms, exhausted but alive. Flower knelt beside them, tears streaming down her face.

The protectors placed their hands over the clearing, sealing it with a glow that faded into the earth. "It is over," they said. "For now."

As the sun rose, warmth spread across the land. Vaughan smiled faintly, knowing this was not the end of her story. But for the first time in what felt like forever, she felt free.

5

THE ESCAPE

On the long drive to the new townhouse, each mile carried them farther from the ashes of the old one. The second property sat on the outskirts of a quiet neighborhood, hidden behind tall evergreens. It was smaller, but as they pulled into the driveway, Vaughan felt a strange sense of relief.

"This is it," she whispered as Eli parked.

Flower stepped out first, her arms folded, scanning the area with narrowed eyes. "At least it's away from the chaos," she muttered, though her tone lacked its usual bite. She had fought hard, and her energy was low.

The house was simple but sturdy. The front door creaked when Eli opened it, revealing bare walls and clean rooms that smelled of cedar. Vaughan walked through the halls slowly, her fingertips brushing against the walls.

They carried in the essentials they'd saved. Eli helped arrange the furniture while Vaughan placed her journals on a shelf and her photo frames on the mantel. It wasn't the old house, but it was something to rebuild from.

The shard was locked in a steel box and placed in the attic, away from daily sight. Even so, Vaughan could still feel its faint pulse, a reminder that their battle was not truly over.

Flower lit protective herbs in every room, filling the house with an earthy, calming scent. For the first time, she didn't criticize Eli's presence. Instead, she worked alongside him in silence.

When night came, they ate together at the new kitchen table. For a brief moment, it felt almost normal—three survivors sharing a meal, the air calm and still.

After dinner, Flower pulled Vaughan aside. "I misjudged him," she said softly, glancing toward Eli. "He's not the cause. He's a shield. Maybe you need him in this."

Vaughan smiled faintly, touched by her mother's words. "I do. But I need you too."

Flower hugged her tightly, and for the first time in years, there was no barrier between them.

Days passed, and the house settled into a routine. Eli stayed in the guest room but spent most of his time helping Vaughan secure the property —reinforcing windows, adding protective charms to the thresholds.

The bad omens stopped. The air was light. For the first time in months, Vaughan slept through the night without nightmares.

She began to believe they had truly won.

But small things reminded her the darkness was never far. The shard's pulse never stopped completely. Some mornings, she swore she heard whispers in the attic, too soft to make out.

One evening, while unpacking the last box, Vaughan found an old photo from the first townhouse. In the background of the picture— barely visible—was the silhouette of the woman, standing in the corner. She dropped the photo, her heart racing.

Eli came to her side instantly. "What is it?"

She picked up the frame, showing him. "She was there . . . even then."

Eli studied the image, his jaw tightening. "She's been watching you longer than we thought."

Flower overheard and walked closer, her face pale. "Then this isn't over. It never was."

That night, Vaughan stood at the balcony, looking out at the quiet street. The moon hung high, bathing the neighborhood in silver light. For a while, she allowed herself to breathe and feel the calm.

But as she turned to go inside, she saw it—just for a moment—across the street under the trees. A tall shadow stood watching her, still as stone. Its eyes glowed faintly.

When she blinked, it was gone.

Vaughan closed the balcony door, locking it with trembling hands. She didn't wake Eli or say a word to Flower. She simply went to bed, heart pounding.

Because deep down, she knew the truth. They had won a battle, not the war.

The next morning, the sun rose over the new townhouse, casting long shadows across the street. To any passerby, it looked peaceful, ordinary. But to Vaughan, every shadow was a reminder that some things never truly fade.

And somewhere, far beyond what they could see, the darkness stirred.

It was waiting. Watching. Preparing.

After weeks of chaos, the new townhouse became a cocoon of safety. The walls no longer hummed with restless energy, and the air no longer carried whispers. For Vaughan, this felt like a fragile slice of normalcy—a gift she wasn't sure she deserved but one she clung to desperately.

Eli stayed, not because he had to, but because he wanted to. He never said it outright, but Vaughan sensed it in the way he hovered protectively, fixing things around the house, making coffee in the mornings, and quietly guarding the attic where the shard was buried.

Flower had changed too, though she wasn't under their roof. She returned to her own home after everything that had happened, but she called often, her voice softer than it had been in years. Sometimes she visited, bringing protective herbs and charms. More often, Vaughan imagined her in meditation, candles flickering around her, or at the table scribbling protective sigils on paper. Her mother had always dabbled in spirituality, but now she was fully immersed in it. The experience had sharpened her gifts and softened her pride.

One sunny afternoon, Eli leaned against the doorway while Vaughan unpacked the last of her boxes. "You've been through hell," he said quietly. "We both have. You need to breathe. We need to breathe."

Vaughan glanced up, tilting her head. "Breathe?"

"Get away for a while. Somewhere quiet. Somewhere without . . . shadows." His voice was calm, but his eyes carried a weight of unspoken things.

She smiled faintly. "Are you asking me on a trip?"

He smirked. "I'm asking you to take a break from saving the world."

The suggestion felt so simple it was almost foreign. And yet, she agreed.

They drove to a lake two hours away, a serene place hidden between towering pines. The water was so clear it mirrored the sky, and the only sound was the gentle lap of waves. They spent the day walking along the shore, talking about everything and nothing—books they'd read, childhood memories, the scars they didn't show anyone else.

Eli shared stories from his past—how he had trained himself to fight long before he ever knew he'd need those skills, how he had lost people to darkness long before meeting her.

Vaughan listened intently, then spoke of her dreams and the intuition that had always guided her.

By sunset, they sat on the hood of the car, watching the sky turn gold and then violet. For the first time in weeks, Vaughan laughed freely. The sound startled her—it had been so long since she heard it.

When they returned home that night, the world felt gentler. For a few days, they lived in that gentleness. Vaughan cooked. Eli fixed the leaky faucet. Flower checked in often, her voice always carrying a warning or a prayer, but she let them have their space. There were no omens or nightmares.

Then one morning, while sipping tea by the window, Vaughan's vision blurred. The steam from her cup swirled, forming into something solid—a golden ticket. It shimmered in her mind's eye, radiating warmth and power. She blinked, and it vanished, leaving her heart pounding.

That night, Eli asked her if she wanted to go out again. "Somewhere new this time," he said with a soft smile. "I like being around you."

She agreed, touched by the sincerity in his voice.

They drove to a quiet café on the edge of town. The evening was peaceful—until two men in suits appeared out of nowhere. Their faces were hidden behind oxygen masks, their presence unnerving and sharp.

Before Vaughan could react, they grabbed Eli, shoving him against the wall. "Where is it?" one demanded.

Eli fought back with brutal precision, knocking one to the ground. "Vaughan, run!" he shouted.

"I'm not leaving you!" she cried, frozen between fear and defiance.

His eyes locked on hers, fierce. "You have to do what I say. Run now!"

Tears stung her eyes as she turned and bolted down the street. Her hands shook as she fumbled with her phone, calling Flower. "Mom—they took Eli!" she sobbed.

She turned back once, hoping to see him, but when she reached the spot, the men—and Eli—were gone.

～

Hours later, when she returned home, she found him standing at her door. His shirt was torn, his face bruised, but his eyes burned with something stronger than pain.

He didn't explain how he escaped, only said, "I'm here."

Inside, they said nothing. They were too exhausted to speak. Eli took the couch, insisting she rest. But as the night stretched on, Vaughan wandered into the living room, startled to find him awake.

She wore a short white nighty made of cotton and sustainable lace, a garment she had forgotten about until tonight. The way his eyes softened when he saw her made her heart race.

She hesitated, but he patted the spot next to him. "Sit."

The air between them was electric, charged with everything they had held back. She sat, their shoulders brushing. He leaned in, and their lips met in a kiss that felt inevitable—gentle at first, then deep, consuming.

His hand slid to her thigh, gripping softly, grounding her in the moment. Her breath hitched, her body trembling, not with fear, but with release.

The world narrowed to just the two of them. Their intimacy was not just physical—it was spiritual, necessary, a merging of everything they had endured and everything they had yet to face.

The moment felt like a storm breaking into sunlight—raw and transformative. For the first time, Vaughan felt truly alive.

The morning after their intimate night was bathed in golden light. Vaughan stirred awake, sunlight spilling through the blinds like warm threads weaving across the room. The air felt different— lighter, yet charged with something unseen.

She walked into the living room, expecting Eli to have left for supplies, but he was still there, stretched out on the couch, asleep. His features were softened by the glow of morning, making him look almost vulnerable—so different from the night before. For a moment, she simply stood, letting herself take him in.

When he opened his eyes, catching her watching, he gave a faint, tired smile. "Morning."

"Morning," she replied, returning the smile, a quiet warmth settling over them.

Neither of them spoke about what had happened between them. They didn't need to. It was there, lingering in every glance, in the way they moved around each other with a new kind of closeness.

The day passed peacefully. Vaughan cooked breakfast, Eli fixed the crooked window latch, and the world outside seemed to slow. For the first time in weeks, there were no whispers or shadows pressing against the walls.

Flower didn't live with them, but she remained a constant presence through her calls and visits. When she phoned that morning, her voice carried a rare softness. "You sound lighter."

Vaughan hesitated, her heart fluttering with secrets she wasn't ready to share. "Things feel . . . calm."

Her mother hummed knowingly. "Stay open to it. There's a reason this peace feels different."

After the call, Vaughan stepped onto the balcony, letting the breeze tangle her hair. The world shimmered for a moment, and suddenly she wasn't there anymore—at least not in her mind. She stood in a vast hall glowing with golden light, a throne gleaming at the far end. She heard faint whispers, voices that felt ancient, and then the vision snapped away.

She gasped, gripping the railing. This wasn't just a dream—it was a message.

That night, she told Eli about the vision. "I keep seeing things . . . not just the golden ticket anymore. There's a throne. It feels like it's calling to me."

Eli's expression darkened. "You're connected to something bigger than you realize."

She searched his eyes. "You know something, don't you?"

He looked away. "Not enough to explain. But I'll find out."

Over the following days, her visions intensified. The golden ticket appeared everywhere—in dreams and in the shapes of the clouds. Each time it shimmered, she felt it was leading her to something important, something life-changing.

Eli grew quieter, making discreet phone calls at night, stepping outside so she wouldn't overhear. Vaughan pretended not to notice, but suspicion coiled tight in her chest.

One evening, while they were sitting at the table eating a simple dinner, he said, "You trust me, right?"

She blinked at him, caught off guard. "Of course."

"Then stay close to me. No matter what happens."

Before she could ask what he meant, a knock sounded at the door. When Eli opened it, two men in black suits and oxygen masks stood there. Their presence radiated danger.

They didn't wait to be invited in—they shoved past Eli, one of them snarling, "Where is it?"

Vaughan froze. The men moved with sharp precision like trained hunters. Eli fought back, his movements brutal and efficient, but they were ready for him.

He gritted his teeth, holding one in a chokehold long enough to yell, "Vaughan, run!"

"I'm not leaving you!" she cried, panic tearing through her.

His eyes burned with fierce command. "You have to do what I say. Run now!"

Tears blurred her vision as she forced herself to flee. Her legs carried her blindly into the night, her hands shaking as she fumbled with her phone. She called her mother. "Mom—they're here! They took Eli!" she sobbed into the receiver.

"Get somewhere safe!" Flower's voice trembled through the line. "Stay hidden. I'm coming to you."

When Vaughan turned back toward the street, the men—and Eli —were gone.

Hours later, after stumbling home in shock, she found him standing at her door. His shirt was torn and his face bruised, but his eyes were alight with something unbroken.

She rushed to him, tears streaming. "You're here."

"I told you I'd always come back," he whispered.

Inside, they said nothing. The silence between them spoke louder than words. Eli took the couch, insisting she rest, but sleep wouldn't come. Hours later, she drifted out of her room and into the living room.

He was still awake, sitting in the dark. His bruises were visible in the slivers of moonlight across his skin. She hesitated at first, standing in the doorway.

When he looked at her, his eyes softened, but they also burned. "Sit with me," he said.

Their lips met, slow and deep, as though they'd been holding back for far too long. His hand gripped her softly, grounding her. She trembled—not from fear but from release.

When it was over, they stayed wrapped in each other's arms, the night silent around them.

Vaughan closed her eyes, and for the first time, her dreams were not of darkness, and there was a throne calling her name. "You are the heir. You must claim it."

The morning after her dream of the golden hall, Vaughan woke with the sensation that the vision hadn't ended. The sunlight streaming through the blinds was brighter than usual, almost blinding, and for a brief second she thought she saw faint symbols etched into the light itself. They vanished as soon as she blinked.

She pressed her hand to her chest. The words from the dream— *You are the heir. You must claim it.*—echoed in her mind like a haunting melody.

When she came into the living room, Eli was already awake,

sipping black coffee. The bruises on his face were fading, but there was a deeper tension in his eyes.

"You didn't sleep," she said softly.

"I couldn't," he said, setting down the mug. "I was thinking about the vision you told me. It's not just random imagery. It's a message."

Vaughan crossed her arms. "From who?"

Eli hesitated, his jaw tightening. "From your ancestors. From the line you carry."

She sat down, the weight of his words sinking in. "You're saying they're trying to guide me?"

"Yes," he said firmly. "And the golden ticket you keep seeing—it's not just a symbol. It's an invitation to claim what's yours."

Before she could ask more, her phone rang. Flower's name flashed on the screen.

"Mom?"

"Vaughan," Flower said, her voice trembling with urgency, "you need to listen to me. I've been researching our lineage. There's an ancient prophecy tied to our bloodline."

Vaughan's heart thudded. "What prophecy?"

"It says when the last heir awakens, the world between worlds will shift. The heir will either restore balance—or unleash chaos," Flower said. "You're that heir. You were always meant to rise, but darkness has been trying to stop you before you realize who you are."

The words hung heavy in the air. Eli met Vaughan's eyes, his jaw set.

"Mom," Vaughan whispered, "what does the golden ticket mean?"

"It's a marker," Flower said. "It appears only to the chosen heir. It's the key to the place where you'll either claim your crown or lose it forever."

Vaughan's fingers trembled. "And where is this place?"

"That's what I don't know," Flower admitted. "But I'm close to finding it."

After the call ended, Vaughan leaned back, her heart racing. "This is bigger than I thought."

Eli crouched beside her. "It always was. You're not just running from them, Vaughan—you're running toward your destiny."

Over the next few days, Flower sent them fragments of old texts, ancient drawings depicting a young woman with a crown of light and a blade made of gold. Vaughan couldn't help but feel that the woman in those sketches was her.

Meanwhile, Eli became even more protective. He rarely left her side, and when he did, it was only to gather information from contacts he refused to name. One evening, she confronted him.

"You know more than you're telling me," she said.

His jaw tightened. "I'm part of something bigger too. An order sworn to protect your bloodline. I've been watching you for years, Vaughan—long before you knew any of this."

Her breath caught. "Why didn't you tell me?"

"Because it wasn't time. And because telling you too soon would've put you in more danger."

That night, the golden ticket appeared again, glowing brighter than ever in her dream. This time, she reached out to touch it, and when her fingers brushed its surface, a door opened—revealing a world of gold and shadow. Beyond it, she saw her throne, but it was guarded by a dark figure who hissed her name.

She woke up gasping, her hands trembling.

When she told Eli, his expression hardened. "The enemy is getting desperate. They know you're close to awakening fully."

The sound of glass shattering ripped through the townhouse. Two masked men stormed inside, moving with deadly precision.

Eli grabbed Vaughan, pushing her behind him. "Stay low!" he barked.

The men lunged, and Eli fought with the ferocity of someone who had been trained for this moment. Vaughan crawled to safety, but one of the men grabbed her arm, yanking her back.

She screamed, kicking and twisting until Eli slammed into the attacker, breaking his grip. The second man swung a weapon, but Eli disarmed him in seconds, forcing both men to retreat.

When it was over, Vaughan collapsed against the wall, shaking.

Eli crouched beside her, cupping her face in his hands. "You're okay. I've got you."

Tears welled in her eyes. "They won't stop."

"No," he said, his voice low, "but neither will I."

After the attack, Flower came to the townhouse, bringing stronger protections. She didn't stay—she never stayed—but she lingered longer than usual, drawing ancient runes on the doors and windows.

"They're not just after you," she said quietly to Vaughan. "They're after what you're meant to become."

That night, Vaughan sat alone in the living room, staring at the steel box that held the shard. She could feel it pulsing, almost humming to her.

When Eli came in, she whispered, "Do you ever feel like we're just pieces on someone else's board?"

He sat beside her. "Maybe. But pieces can become something more. You're not a pawn, Vaughan. You're the queen they're trying to stop from taking her place."

The air between them thickened, not with fear, but with understanding.

Later, as the moon rose high, Vaughan drifted into another vision. This time, the golden ticket floated into her hand. The whispers around her grew louder, forming words: "Follow the path. Claim the light. You are the last empress."

When she woke, she knew her journey was only beginning.

The night after Flower left, the townhouse felt unsettlingly quiet. Vaughan sat curled up on the couch, her knees drawn to her chest, staring at the shadows stretching across the floor. There was no whispering this time, no direct threat, but the silence itself felt like a predator waiting to strike.

Eli entered from the kitchen, a glass of water in his hand. He studied her for a long moment. "You're not sleeping," he said, his voice soft but edged with concern.

"How can I?" Her voice trembled. "Every time I close my eyes, I see it. The golden ticket—it's everywhere now. It's like it's calling me."

He placed the glass on the table and sat beside her. "That's because it is. But it's not ready to reveal everything yet. And neither are you."

She turned to him, frustration building. "Then why show me at all? Why torment me with glimpses I can't understand?"

"Because it wants you to look," Eli said simply. "To seek. To remember."

The word *remember* echoed in her mind.

❧

The following morning, Vaughan found herself drawn to her grandmother's book—the one Flower had brought. She sat at the table, flipping through its brittle pages. The text was written in an archaic language, but certain words seemed to vibrate against the paper.

She traced her finger over a passage that stood out: *The heir will see the key not in what is shown, but in what is hidden.*

Her breath hitched. "Hidden . . ." she murmured.

Eli walked in, his hair damp from the shower, his expression unreadable. "You found something?"

"Maybe," she whispered, tapping the page. "It's saying the answers are hidden—but where?"

He leaned over, his presence warm but commanding. "Don't force it. The more you chase it, the more it will slip away. Let it come to you."

❧

That afternoon, Flower called again, her voice sharp and urgent. "I had another vision," she said. "The golden ticket appeared, but it wasn't just floating this time—it was locked in something, surrounded by symbols I couldn't recognize."

"Locked?" Vaughan asked, her pulse quickening.

"Yes," Flower said. "And when I tried to reach for it, the vision shifted. I saw a figure cloaked in shadow, standing between you and the ticket. It spoke, but I couldn't hear the words."

The call left Vaughan shaken. She felt the walls of her world closing in, as though time itself was running out.

That night, she had another dream. This time, the golden ticket hovered above a stone pedestal in a room filled with light and shadow interwoven. She reached for it, but as her fingers brushed its surface, the room cracked like glass, and darkness swallowed everything.

She woke gasping, with a voice echoing in her ear: "You are not ready."

The next morning, Eli found her sitting on the balcony, staring at the horizon. "What did you see?"

She swallowed hard. "The ticket. But every time I get close, something stops me. It said I'm not ready."

Eli's expression darkened. "It's testing you. Whatever's guiding it —it won't let you claim it until you've proven yourself."

She shivered, hugging her arms around herself. "How do I prove myself to something I don't understand?"

He crouched beside her, his hand resting gently on hers. "By surviving. By fighting. By trusting yourself."

6

———

THE GOLDEN TICKET

For the next few days, tension coiled tighter around them. They rarely left the house, and when they did, Eli was always hyper-aware, scanning every shadow, every stranger who came too close.

One evening, as Vaughan was cleaning the kitchen, she caught a glimmer in the reflection of the window—a faint outline of the ticket shimmering behind her. When she turned, it vanished. But the reflection lingered in her mind, a reminder that it was always watching her.

Flower came by later that night, her face pale and drawn. "I found something," she said, setting down a stack of old papers. "These are fragments of a map, but they're incomplete. They're tied to the prophecy. I think they lead to where the ticket will fully reveal itself."

Vaughan leaned over the papers. The fragments were covered in cryptic markings, symbols that looked almost alive. "Where does it lead?"

"That's the problem," Flower said, shaking her head. "It's missing pieces. Until you have them, you can't reach it. And the enemy knows that."

Eli stood with his arms crossed, his eyes narrowing. "Which means they'll try to stop her before she finds the rest."

The lights in the townhouse flickered, and a loud crash echoed from outside. Eli moved instantly, motioning for Vaughan to stay back. Through the window, they saw figures moving in the shadows —more hunters, their movements swift and calculated.

Vaughan said, "They're here."

Eli grabbed his weapon, positioning himself near the door. "Stay behind me, no matter what happens."

The hunters stormed the house, their masks reflecting the dim light. The air was filled with the sound of glass breaking and footsteps pounding. Eli fought fiercely, his every movement precise, but there were too many.

One charged toward Vaughan, but she ducked and grabbed a kitchen knife, slashing upward. The man fell back, surprised by her strength.

Eli knocked out the last attacker with brutal force. Blood dripped from his knuckles as he turned to her. "You're getting stronger," he said, almost proud.

She trembled. "They won't stop, will they?"

"No," he said, wiping his face. "Because you're closer to the truth than ever."

After the attackers retreated, Flower reinforced the house with protective wards. Before leaving, she looked Vaughan in the eyes. "Every step you take toward the ticket will make them fight harder. But you can't let fear create the path for you."

That night, Vaughan couldn't sleep. She sat on the couch, knees pulled close, staring at the moon. The golden ticket flashed again in her vision, but this time it didn't just glow—it pulsed like a heartbeat, calling her name.

Eli came out from his room, sitting beside her silently. "You saw it again," he said softly.

She nodded. "It's closer now. I can feel it."

He looked at her, his expression unreadable. "Then whatever's coming . . . it'll be worse than anything we've faced."

She met his gaze, her heart pounding. "And we'll face it together."

Vaughan knew she was walking toward something she didn't yet understand—something that would change everything.

As the night deepened, the shard in the attic pulsed in rhythm with her heartbeat. Somewhere far away, the enemy moved their pieces, preparing for their next strike.

In her dreams, the golden ticket hovered just out of reach, waiting.

The days after the attack felt like living in the eye of a hurricane— eerily calm, yet thick with the knowledge that something larger was gathering force. Vaughan moved through the house like a shadow, her thoughts consumed by the golden ticket, the incomplete map, and the weight of what Eli had told her about her bloodline.

She felt different. Stronger. The bruises she'd gotten during the fight were already fading faster than they should have. When she stood in front of the mirror, she thought her eyes shimmered faintly under certain light, catching a glint that hadn't been there before.

Flower's words echoed in her head: *When the heir awakens, the world between worlds will shift.*

One morning, as she poured water into a glass, the stream bent unnaturally, curling upward as if it were obeying her thoughts. She gasped, stepping back, and the water spilled everywhere.

Eli walked in at that exact moment, catching the tail end of what happened. His eyes narrowed. "You're starting to manifest."

She stared at him, heart pounding. "Manifest?"

"It's your power. It's waking up. And it won't stop now."

That night, Flower came by with the old book and new fragments of information. Her expression was tense, the lines around her eyes deeper. "I found a ritual," she said, spreading out pages on the table. "It's tied to the golden ticket. It's said to reveal the location to the heir, but only if it's done correctly. If it's done wrong . . . "

Eli's jaw tightened. "What does it require?"

Flower hesitated. "Blood. And not just any blood—the heir's. A drop on the shard under the full moon. Only then will the path open."

Vaughan felt a chill crawl up her spine. "And if I do this?"

"It will draw the path to you," Flower said softly. "But it will also draw them."

Eli crossed his arms. "Then we need to prepare for war."

The following days were spent in a blur of training, research, and preparation. Eli pushed Vaughan harder, teaching her to fight not just physically, but with focus—channeling the strange energy she had begun to feel. At first, she resisted, terrified of the power flickering beneath her skin, but soon she learned to harness it, even if only in small bursts.

One night, while practicing in the living room, she raised her hand instinctively to block Eli's strike—and a pulse of energy shot out, throwing him back against the wall.

She froze, horrified. "Eli, I'm sorry!"

He stood, breathing hard but smiling faintly. "Don't be sorry. Be ready to use that when it counts."

Flower, who'd been watching quietly, said, "The more you awaken, the more dangerous this becomes. Remember that."

As the full moon approached, tension grew thicker. The shard in the attic pulsed more violently each night, and the golden ticket appeared more vividly in Vaughan's visions. Sometimes she woke to find faint golden dust on her pillow, as if the visions were bleeding into reality.

Meanwhile, Eli was growing restless. Vaughan caught him

making late-night calls, his voice low and urgent. One evening, she followed him to the porch, where he stood with his back to her.

"Who are you talking to?" she asked.

He turned, startled. "No one you need to worry about."

"Don't lie to me," she said firmly. "You're hiding something."

He exhaled sharply. "It's my order. They're warning me. They say protecting you any further will cost me everything."

Vaughan's stomach dropped. "Cost you what?"

"My life. My standing. Everything I swore to."

She stepped closer, her voice soft but fierce. "And what do you choose?"

He looked at her, and for a moment, all the walls he'd built cracked. "You. Every time, I choose you."

Three nights before the ritual, Flower called with an urgent tone. "The map's symbols are shifting," she said. "I think the pieces are rearranging themselves to form the complete path. But I can't hold them long—something is trying to block me."

As she spoke, the line crackled with static, and Vaughan heard a faint voice whispering her name through the phone. She hung up, trembling.

That same night, shadows gathered outside the townhouse. Eli saw them first, his hand going instinctively to his weapon. "They're here."

The air thickened, and Vaughan felt it—an oppressive energy pressing against the house. Flower's wards held for a while, glowing faintly along the windows, but cracks of darkness seeped through.

"They're stronger this time," Eli muttered.

The hunters moved like a single entity, coordinated and ruthless. Eli fought at the front, his strikes deadly and precise, while Vaughan used the energy inside her, releasing bursts of power that knocked attackers back.

But there were too many of them.

"Vaughan!" Eli shouted, catching one man's blade with his arm before breaking it. "Get to the shard! Use it!"

She hesitated. "It's not the full moon yet!"

"Do it now!"

With no choice, Vaughan ran to the attic, her breath ragged. The shard glowed violently, pulsing in rhythm with her heartbeat. She sliced her palm with a broken piece of glass and let a drop of blood fall onto it.

The shard erupted in light, and a wave of golden energy surged through the house, throwing the hunters back. The darkness shrieked as it retreated, leaving the townhouse shaking but intact.

Eli stumbled into the attic, blood on his shirt, but alive. "You did it," he said, panting.

The shard's light dimmed, leaving behind a single glowing symbol etched into the floor.

Vaughan stared at it and whispered, "What is it?"

Eli knelt beside her. "It's part of the path. The first piece."

The symbol burned faintly on the attic floor long after the light from the shard faded. Vaughan knelt beside it, and the glowing mark shifted subtly. She reached toward it, but Eli's hand caught hers.

"Not yet," he said, his voice sharp. "Touching it now could trigger something we're not ready for."

She withdrew her hand, trembling. "It's . . . beautiful. Terrifying, but beautiful."

"It's a piece of the map," Eli said, still keeping his gaze locked on the symbol. "The ritual worked—but only partially. You'll need to find the other pieces before the path can open completely."

Vaughan wrapped her injured palm with a strip of cloth. "And in the meantime, they'll keep coming."

"They'll never stop," Eli said flatly. "Not until they take you. Or until you claim what's yours."

∽

That night, neither of them slept. The townhouse carried an eerie stillness. The symbol's glow dimmed slowly, but Vaughan felt it pulsing inside her chest, syncing with her heartbeat. She couldn't tell if it was comforting or frightening.

When Flower arrived the next morning, she stopped dead at the sight of the attic. "You've awakened the first seal," she said, her voice trembling.

"Seal?" Vaughan asked.

Flower stepped closer, running her fingers over the faint edges of the glowing mark. "This isn't just a map—it's a seal to keep the power hidden. Each piece you uncover weakens the barriers between your world and what lies beyond."

Vaughan's chest tightened. "What happens when I find them all?"

"You'll either rise as the queen you're meant to be," Flower whispered, "or the darkness will consume you completely."

Later that day, while Vaughan tried to meditate with the symbol in her mind, Eli stepped outside to take a call. She followed quietly, standing just behind the doorway.

"You can't stop me," Eli said. "I'm not abandoning her."

She responded coldly, though Vaughan couldn't make out the words.

Eli's tone turned to steel. "Then do what you have to do. I'll protect her, order or no order."

The call ended abruptly. Eli turned, startled to see her standing there. "You heard that?"

She crossed her arms. "Who was that?"

He hesitated, then said, "The order. They sent a warning—they want me to stand down."

"And you won't," she said, almost as a statement.

"Never," he replied.

That night, Vaughan drifted to sleep on the couch, only to be jolted awake by a violent surge of energy crackling around her. The lamps flickered wildly, and objects vibrated, lifting slightly off the shelves.

Eli ran in, his weapon drawn. "Vaughan, what's happening?"

"I—I don't know!" she cried, clutching her head. Energy surged from her hands uncontrollably, cracking the glass on the windows and sending a lamp crashing to the floor.

Flower rushed in moments later, drawn by the disturbance. She began chanting under her breath, moving toward Vaughan slowly. "You're channeling too much at once! Breathe, focus!"

Vaughan's vision blurred, her body trembling as light poured from her fingertips. She forced herself to take a deep breath, and slowly, the energy calmed, fading into faint sparks that dissipated in the air.

She collapsed into Eli's arms, shaking. "What's happening to me?"

"You're awakening," Flower said grimly. "But you're not in control yet. If you can't learn to control it, the power will destroy you before they even get the chance."

The next day, Eli brought her to an abandoned training ground in the woods. "We can't stay in the house forever," he said. "You need to learn to control what's inside you—and to fight without fear."

Under his guidance, Vaughan practiced channeling her energy. At first, every pulse was wild and unpredictable, scattering rocks and toppling branches. But with each attempt, she grew steadier. By sunset, she could release energy in a focused burst, enough to shatter a tree trunk in a single strike.

She was still catching her breath when a voice called from the trees. "Impressive."

They both spun around, weapons raised. A man stepped out from the shadows, wearing a dark coat adorned with a silver crest. His eyes glowed faintly under the fading light.

Eli tensed. "You."

The man smirked. "So it's true—you've betrayed the order."

Vaughan's heart pounded. "Who are you?"

"Someone who was sent to bring you back into line," the man said coldly. "But I see you've already chosen her over us."

Eli stepped in front of Vaughan. "You're not taking her."

The man tilted his head. "Oh, I'm not here to take her. Not yet. I'm here to warn her."

Vaughan narrowed her eyes. "Warn me about what?"

"The path you're walking is lined with corpses. The closer you get to the truth, the more blood will spill—yours, his, and anyone who dares to help you." His tone sharpened. "Turn back while you can."

"I won't," Vaughan said, her voice steady despite the fear in her chest.

The man studied her for a long moment, then smirked. "Then I'll see you at the end, heir." With that, he vanished into the trees as if swallowed by the shadows.

Eli exhaled slowly. "They're watching us."

"Let them watch," Vaughan said through clenched teeth. "I'm not stopping."

As they headed back to the townhouse, a storm gathered on the horizon. The wind carried whispers, and Vaughan felt the mark in the attic burning faintly, as if responding to something unseen.

That night, she dreamed again—this time, not of the golden ticket itself, but of a voice whispering in the darkness: "The first test comes at . . . at . . . "

She jolted awake, heart pounding, just as the sky lightened outside.

She wanted to know when the test was coming, but woke up before the dream could finish.

Dawn crept slowly across the horizon, the sky bleeding from deep indigo into soft rose. Wisps of clouds drifted like torn silk across the light, and the air carried the scent of dew. Vaughan stood at the window, her breath fogging the glass, eyes fixed on the glowing line where night surrendered to day. The voice from her dream echoed in her mind—*The first test comes at dawn.*

She turned to find Eli already awake, sitting at the edge of the couch, lacing his boots. He glanced up, his expression hard. "You felt it too."

"It wasn't just a dream," she said quietly.

"No," he agreed. "It never is."

Before she could respond, Flower called. Her voice was low and urgent. "Vaughan, listen to me. I woke up to a vision—your test is coming now. You won't be ready if you doubt yourself. Whatever happens, don't let fear take control. Fear feeds them."

Vaughan's hands trembled as she hung up. Eli stood, grabbing his weapons. "Stay close to me, and remember what we practiced."

The first sign of danger came as a ripple through the air, a distortion that made the dawn sky outside shimmer strangely. The golden-pink glow fractured into unnatural streaks, bending like liquid. Vaughan's pulse spiked.

"Here they come," Eli muttered.

The door exploded inward with unnatural force, splintering into shards. Figures stormed in—cloaked, masked, moving unnaturally fast. These weren't ordinary hunters. Their movements were too fluid, almost inhuman.

Eli met them head-on, his strikes sharp and calculated, but they kept coming, slipping through every defense. Vaughan felt her chest tighten with panic. Her power sparked erratically, bursts of light shooting from her hands.

One of the figures charged at her, claws scraping the air. Instinct took over—Vaughan threw her hands up, and a massive wave of energy erupted from her chest, blasting the attacker across the room and shattering the windows. The shattered glass reflected the sunrise outside, scattering shards of light across the floor.

The others hesitated, sensing the surge of her power. Eli yelled, "Control it, Vaughan! Focus!"

But she couldn't. The energy kept building, spiraling out, cracking the floor beneath her feet. The attackers used her lack of control to close in, moving like shadows.

"*No!*" she screamed, releasing everything at once. A blinding explosion of light filled the room, drowning out even the brilliance of the dawn sky beyond the broken windows. The attackers were thrown back, the air vibrating with raw force.

When the light faded, the sky outside had shifted to a fiery canvas, streaked with copper and crimson.

Eli rushed to her side, grabbing her shoulders. "Look at me! You're okay. You did it."

Vaughan was shaking, tears in her eyes. "I couldn't control it. I nearly destroyed everything."

"But you didn't," Eli said firmly. "You survived. That was the test."

Before they could catch their breath, a low hum filled the air. The attackers who had survived began to dissolve into black mist, whispering in unison: "You have passed the first gate. The path opens."

The mist swirled into a vortex, and from it, something materialized—a golden shimmer forming into the shape of a ticket. It hovered midair, glowing faintly before splitting into two pieces. One piece burned an image into Vaughan's mind: A set of ancient ruins bathed in moonlight. The other piece disintegrated into dust.

Vaughan gasped. "I saw it. A place . . . ruins."

Eli's eyes narrowed. "The next clue."

The mark in the attic began to glow in response, brighter than before, as if acknowledging the test was complete.

Flower arrived moments later, skidding to a stop when she saw the damage. Her face was pale. "You awakened part of the path, didn't you?"

"Yes," Vaughan said, still trembling. "The ticket gave me a vision. The ruins—they're calling me."

Flower touched her arm, her voice firm. "Then this was only the beginning. The next step will be harder."

Later that evening, after cleaning the wreckage, Vaughan sat with Eli on the porch. The sun was setting now, painting the sky in streaks of violet and bronze, and they were surrounded by the scent of rain yet to fall. The silence between them was heavy but not uncomfortable. She stared at the horizon, where the last traces of sunlight lingered.

"Why do I feel like the more power I use, the less of me there is?" she whispered.

Eli looked at her, his expression softening. "Because power changes you. The trick is holding onto who you are while wielding it."

She nodded, her gaze drifting back to the horizon. "I don't know if I can."

"You can," he said. "I've seen you fight through worse."

As darkness fell, Eli's phone buzzed. He stepped away to answer it, his tone sharp and clipped. Vaughan caught only fragments: ". . . she passed . . . no, I won't hand her over . . . you'll have to go through me."

When he returned, his expression was grim. "They're sending someone else. Someone stronger."

"Who?" she asked.

"The order's top enforcer. If he comes, it means they've decided you're too dangerous to live."

Vaughan's blood ran cold. "And you?"

"I'll stand against them," he said without hesitation.

That night, as Vaughan drifted into an uneasy sleep, the golden ticket appeared again—this time shrouded in shadows. A voice whispered: "The ruins hold your crown. But the crown will not accept the unworthy."

She woke with a start, her chest tight. She knew what she had to do next.

But she also knew the enemy was getting closer with every step she took.

The night stretched long and uneasy. Even after the attack, after the mist whispered its cryptic promise, Vaughan couldn't rest. When sleep finally claimed her, it wasn't the usual golden hall or the familiar whispers.

This time, she found herself standing in a desolate courtyard. The ground was cracked, vines crawling across broken stone. The sky above was a color she couldn't name, shifting between bruised purple and sickly green. Around her, statues of faceless figures stared down, their mouths opening silently as if screaming without sound.

At the center, the golden ticket floated—not glowing, but decaying, its edges crumbling to ash. Vaughan stepped toward it, but with every step, the statues moved, turning their heads to follow her.

One statue reached out, its stone fingers cracking open. Its voice was gravel, rough and low:

"Every step forward costs you something."

The ticket disintegrated completely, and darkness swallowed her whole.

She woke gasping, drenched in cold sweat. Eli sat in the chair beside her, alert despite the late hour. "Another vision?"

She nodded, her voice trembling. "It was different this time. Wrong. The ticket—it crumbled."

Eli leaned forward. "That's not just a vision. It's a warning. If you lose control, the path will close."

By morning, Flower called with an urgent tone. "Vaughan, something's happening. My visions are . . . fractured. I keep seeing pieces of the map rearranging themselves into shapes—then collapsing. There's something tampering with the prophecy."

"What do you mean?" Vaughan asked.

"I mean something is rewriting it," Flower said. "You're not just fighting them—you're fighting time itself. Something doesn't want this path to exist anymore."

That day, Vaughan experienced another vision—not while sleeping, but in broad daylight. As she sipped tea, the steam rose unnaturally, twisting into swirling patterns. Inside the mist, she saw flashes: A black crown dripping with tar, a forest of trees with hollow faces carved into them, a river flowing backward with hands reaching out from beneath its surface.

The images struck her like a cold blade, vanishing as quickly as they came. She dropped the cup, porcelain shattering. Eli caught her as she staggered back.

"They're getting inside my head," she whispered.

"No," Eli said, gripping her arms. "You're seeing things no one else can. That's not weakness—it's part of what makes you the heir."

Later that evening, as dusk settled, the air grew unnaturally still. Even the birds outside had gone silent. Vaughan and Eli exchanged a glance, both sensing it at the same time: They weren't alone.

A figure approached the house, cloaked in black with a silver emblem that shimmered faintly even in the dying light. His presence was suffocating, every step deliberate. Eli moved to the door, weapon in hand.

"Stay back," he warned Vaughan.

The man stepped inside as if invited, his voice calm and deep. "You've strayed far, Eli. You were sworn to the order. And now you protect the very thing you were meant to deliver."

Eli's grip tightened on his weapon. "I told you—I won't hand her over."

The man's eyes glowed faintly beneath his hood. "Then you're a traitor. And you know what happens to traitors."

Vaughan stepped forward despite Eli's warning. "Who are you?"

The man tilted his head. "You may call me Kaelen. I am here to give you a choice." His gaze pierced her. "Come with me willingly, and I'll ensure your path is unhindered. Resist, and everyone you love will suffer for your stubbornness."

Vaughan's heart pounded. "I'm not going anywhere with you."

Kaelen smirked. "You have spirit. That will make the end sweeter."

He vanished into shadow, but his presence lingered, leaving the house colder than before.

Eli slammed the door. "That was their top enforcer. If he's here, things are about to get worse."

That night, Vaughan's visions grew relentless. Each time she closed her eyes, she was somewhere new:

A hallway lined with mirrors where her own reflection laughed back at her, each version twisted in a different way.

A field of golden flowers that turned black and brittle when she touched them.

A staircase spiraling upward into darkness, with whispers urging her to keep climbing.

Each vision left her shaken, her powers sparking erratically. The walls flickered with faint golden light every time her emotions surged.

By morning, Flower arrived with trembling hands clutching the old book. "The second seal has appeared in my visions. It's hidden within a place of silence—where no sound can survive. But Kaelen is also searching for it. If he finds it first—"

"He won't," Eli said.

They spent the day planning. Vaughan packed essentials while Flower marked protective symbols on her skin. Eli checked his weapons with silent determination.

When night fell, they set out toward the location Flower described. The forest surrounding the path was unnaturally quiet, every leaf and branch coated in a strange stillness. Even their footsteps sounded muffled.

Halfway through the woods, the silence shattered. Shadows lunged from the trees, their movements jerky and unnatural. Eli fought them off with precision, but more kept coming, swarming.

Vaughan's powers surged wildly, bursts of energy shooting from her hands, but the attackers twisted around her strikes. One grabbed her wrist, and as it touched her, a new vision flashed—Kaelen standing at the ruins, holding the golden ticket. His eyes burned with victory.

She screamed, releasing a surge of power so violent it sent every attacker flying back into the trees. The blast left the ground scorched.

When the dust settled, the forest was silent again.

Vaughan collapsed to her knees, panting. Eli knelt beside her. "You're getting stronger. But it's costing you."

Before she could respond, a golden shimmer appeared ahead of them—hovering like a firefly. It wasn't the ticket itself, but a fragment of it, swirling with both light and shadow. It floated toward her, then dissolved into her chest, leaving behind a burning sensation.

Flower's eyes widened. "The ticket has chosen you again. The second seal is near."

But as they pressed forward, Vaughan knew Larzine was already closing in, and the next step would demand more from her than she had ever given.

The forest grew stranger the deeper they went. At first, it was only the quiet—so deep it felt unnatural. Then the trees began to change. Their trunks twisted upward, hollow eyes carved into the bark, as if they had witnessed centuries of secrets and were now watching Vaughan pass through.

Every step they took muffled into the earth. Even the wind seemed caught, frozen mid-breath. Vaughan glanced at Eli, who gripped his weapon tightly, scanning the trees. Flower followed close behind, clutching a bundle of herbs and protective charms, her lips moving silently in prayer.

"This is it," Flower whispered. "The place of silence. Sound dies here."

Indeed, Vaughan realized she couldn't hear her own footsteps anymore. When she spoke, her words came out like a muted hum, as though the forest swallowed them whole.

The mark on her arm—one Flower had drawn for protection—glowed faintly, casting soft light on the path ahead.

As they moved forward, a fog rolled in, low and thick, curling around their ankles. Shapes flickered within it—shadows moving too quickly to follow. Were they real or just tricks of the mist?

Then, the fog thinned, revealing an open clearing. At its center stood an ancient stone archway, cracked but still standing. It pulsed faintly with golden veins that ran across its surface like living roots.

"The seal is there," Flower mouthed, pointing to the arch.

Vaughan stepped forward, drawn to it, when a ripple of energy shot through the clearing. Her vision blurred. The arch dissolved, and she was somewhere else entirely—standing in a hall of mirrors, the same eerie place from one of her earlier dreams.

But this time, the mirrors didn't reflect her; they reflected hundreds of versions of Larzine, each watching her with cold, glowing eyes. One of the reflections stepped forward, speaking in a voice that came from everywhere at once: "You cannot reach the seal without bleeding for it."

The mirror shattered, and Vaughan fell to her knees, snapping back into reality. Eli grabbed her, his eyes sharp with concern. "What happened?"

"They're inside my head," she gasped. "Larzine is everywhere."

A loud crack split the air, shattering the unnatural silence. Figures emerged from the mist, cloaked like before, but these were different. Their forms wavered like smoke, their eyes glowing faint gold. They weren't hunters. They were something older.

"They're guardians," Flower said, her voice trembling. "They protect the seal from anyone unworthy."

The guardians advanced without hesitation. Eli stepped in front of Vaughan, but she pushed past him. "No—I have to do this."

Her hands sparked with golden light as the guardians charged. Energy burst from her fingertips, but instead of knocking them back, it split into ribbons of light that wrapped around the figures, freezing them mid-stride.

The archway pulsed brighter in response. Vaughan stepped

closer, each movement heavy as if she were walking through water. Her vision wavered again—this time, she stood at the ruins from her earlier vision, the moon glowing like a silver blade above. Larzine was there, standing at the archway, his expression unreadable.

"Every step costs you something," he whispered again, his voice like smoke. "Are you willing to pay?"

When she blinked, the ruins vanished, and she was back in the clearing. Without hesitation, Vaughan drew a blade Eli handed her, cutting her palm. Her blood dripped onto the base of the arch, sinking into the stone.

The ground trembled. The archway flared with golden light, and a second symbol appeared, burning into its surface. The guardians dissolved into mist.

Vaughan collapsed to her knees. Eli caught her, holding her tightly. "You did it."

But the moment of relief was short-lived. The air rippled, and Larzine stepped out of the shadows, his cloak flowing unnaturally.

"You're stronger than I expected," he said softly, almost with admiration. "But you're not ready to face what comes next."

Eli stepped in front of Vaughan, his weapon raised. "You're not touching her."

Larzine smirked. "Brave. Foolish." He lifted his hand, and the shadows around him surged, forming into tendrils that lashed toward Eli.

Eli blocked, but Larzine was fast, moving like a phantom. Their fight erupted into a blur of strikes and energy, sparks flying as steel clashed with shadow. Vaughan tried to stand, but the ritual had weakened her too much.

Flower grabbed her arm. "Not yet. You'll die if you move now."

Vaughan's eyes burned as she watched Eli being pushed back. Then, something inside her snapped. The mark on her arm flared, and golden energy erupted from her body, shooting outward like a shockwave.

Larzine staggered but didn't fall. Instead, he smiled. "Yes. That's it. That's the power I want to see."

With a swirl of shadow, he vanished, his voice lingering: "The final seal will break soon. When it does, only one of us will claim it."

The clearing fell silent once again. The archway glowed faintly, its new symbol shining like a star.

Vaughan collapsed into Eli's arms, whispering, "We have to reach the final seal before he does."

Eli held her close, his voice steady despite the chaos. "Then we move fast. There's no turning back now."

7

———

THE FIGHT AT DAWN

They left the place of silence at dawn, the archway's glow fading behind them as the forest returned to its unsettling stillness. Vaughan leaned heavily on Eli as they walked, the cut on her palm throbbing where her blood had sealed the second gate. Flower followed in silence, her eyes distant, as if she were still half in the world of visions.

The deeper they went into the forest, the more Vaughan felt something following them—not Larzine, not the hunters, but something else. The trees seemed to lean closer, the branches creaking though there was no wind.

When they finally emerged onto open ground, the sun was rising, its golden light fractured by clouds. Vaughan paused, her eyes drawn to the horizon where the sky seemed to shimmer faintly—as if something beyond it was watching.

That night, they found shelter in an abandoned chapel on the edge of a deserted village. The walls were cracked, ivy creeping over the broken windows, and an altar stood covered in dust.

Eli secured the doors while Flower lit candles, placing them in a circle around Vaughan. "You need rest," Flower said. "Your body's recovering, but your spirit is ahead of you. If you collapse now, you'll never make it to the last seal."

Vaughan sat in the circle, the candlelight casting long, flickering shadows on the walls. She closed her eyes, and almost instantly, visions flooded her.

She was standing on a bridge made of glass, stretching over an abyss. Beneath the glass, faces screamed silently, their mouths open wide, their eyes burning gold. Ahead of her, the golden ticket floated —but this time, its glow was corrupted by veins of black spreading across it.

She stepped forward, and the glass cracked. The faces beneath pressed harder against it, their whispers filling her head: "Not all who claim the crown survive it."

The bridge shattered, and she plummeted into the abyss.

When she opened her eyes, she was back in the chapel, gasping for air. The candles around her had burned almost to stubs. Eli knelt beside her, his hand gripping hers. "What did you see?"

She swallowed hard. "The crown . . . it's changing. There's something corrupting it."

Flower's voice trembled. "That means Larzine is close. He's trying to twist the path before you reach it."

Eli's jaw tightened. "Then we need to move faster."

Before they could plan their next move, the chapel's door creaked open. A man stepped inside, his presence as cold as the winter wind. He wore the same silver crest as Larzine, but his eyes were colder.

Eli stiffened, stepping between Vaughan and the man. "You shouldn't be here."

The man smirked. "Neither should you. You've gone against the order, Eli. You know what that means."

"I don't care," Eli growled. "I'm not handing her over."

The man tilted his head. "You've already been marked for death. When the final seal breaks, you'll fall with her."

Vaughan stood, her hands sparking with faint golden light. "Leave us."

The man chuckled. "You have fire, heir. Let's see how long it lasts." He stepped back into the shadows, vanishing without another word.

Eli exhaled slowly, his hands shaking slightly. "They're closing in. They won't stop until one of us is dead."

Flower approached, her face pale. "I've seen it—the final seal. It's hidden where time stands still, where night and day collide. But it's not just a place. It's a test unlike anything you've faced."

Vaughan said, "And if I fail?"

Flower looked away. "You'll lose more than your life. You'll lose yourself."

That night, Vaughan dreamed again. This vision was different—more real than any before. She stood in a hall lined with torches that burned black. At the end, Larzine waited, sitting on a throne of shadow. The golden ticket floated above his hand, twisting into shapes she couldn't comprehend.

He smiled faintly. "You think you can stop me? You've only unlocked doors for me to walk through."

She tried to move toward him, but the floor cracked beneath her feet, revealing a chasm filled with golden fire. The voices from the abyss rose louder, screaming her name.

Larzine stood, stepping into the flames without burning. "When the final seal breaks, only one of us will rise. Prepare yourself, heir. I will be waiting."

The vision ended with a blinding flash of light, and Vaughan woke with a cry.

Eli was already at her side, his eyes searching hers. "Another vision?"

She nodded. "He's waiting for me at the last seal. He's not afraid—he's ready."

Eli's grip tightened. "Then so are we."

As dawn broke, Flower prepared the final set of symbols, painting them across Vaughan's skin. "You will need everything you have," she whispered. "The last seal will demand it."

Vaughan looked at Eli, her chest tight. "Whatever happens, we go together."

He nodded, his voice low but firm. "Together."

The sky above them churned as they stepped out of the chapel, streaked with both gold and shadow—as if the world itself was split between light and darkness.

They began their journey toward the final seal, unaware of the horrors waiting for them. But as they walked, Vaughan felt something deep inside her shift. Her power burned brighter, her visions sharper, and her destiny heavier than ever.

Somewhere far ahead, Larzine waited, the crown of shadow gleaming faintly in the void.

And the path to the final seal had already begun to open.

The journey to the last seal began under a sky that never settled. The clouds shifted unnaturally, colors bleeding into one another—gold, violet, and streaks of shadow that writhed like living things. The air was thick with energy that crackled against Vaughan's skin.

For hours, they walked through landscapes that felt wrong. Rivers flowed upward, their surfaces reflecting not the sky, but faces Vaughan had seen in her dreams—faces twisted in silent warning.

Every step forward pressed on her mind. Her visions bled into reality, flashes appearing before her eyes without warning:

The golden ticket nailed to a cross, dripping molten gold.

A young version of herself running through endless corridors, chased by faceless figures.

The crown of light cracking, pieces scattering like stars, only to reform into something darker.

Each vision left her breathless, her hands trembling with surges of uncontrolled power.

Eli walked close beside her, his gaze sharp. "The seal's close. I can feel it."

Flower lagged behind, clutching a talisman, whispering prayers under her breath. "We're crossing into the place where night and day collide. Be ready—the veil here is thin."

By dusk, they reached a plateau where the sun and moon hung side by side in the same sky, frozen. In the center of the plateau stood an obsidian gate, its surface swirling with shadows and faint veins of gold.

"This is it," Flower whispered.

Vaughan stepped forward, her chest tight. The moment her foot touched the stone ground before the gate, the world shattered.

The sky fractured into shards of light, and she was pulled into a void where there was no up or down—only an endless expanse of darkness streaked with gold. She stood alone at first, then voices echoed: "Claim it. Claim what is yours."

The darkness coalesced, and Larzine appeared, his cloak billowing unnaturally, his eyes glowing with power. Behind him, the golden ticket hovered, corrupted by veins of black energy twisting through it.

"You finally made it," he said, his voice smooth yet venomous. "The last heir. The last obstacle."

"This ends now," Vaughan said, her voice shaking but strong.

Larzine raised a hand, and the shadows surged, forming into jagged weapons that sliced through the void. Vaughan dodged, barely controlling the golden energy bursting from her hands. The two forces collided—light against shadow—each strike sending shock-waves that fractured the space around them.

Eli said, "Vaughan! Focus!" He was there now, fighting off shadow creatures that poured from the darkness.

The battle raged, every moment more intense than the last. Larzine's power was overwhelming, bending the void to his will. But Vaughan's light burned brighter, each surge stronger than before.

"You're powerful," Larzine said with a twisted smile, "but power without control is destruction."

She gritted her teeth, forcing her energy to focus into a single, blinding beam. The light struck him, tearing through his shadow armor, forcing him to his knees. The golden ticket floated between them, torn between light and shadow.

"This isn't over," Larzine hissed, vanishing into darkness. "The crown will decide."

The void collapsed, and Vaughan found herself back at the gate, the ticket hovering above her palm. It pulsed, pure gold again—but fragile, as if one wrong move could shatter it.

Flower rushed to her side, tears in her eyes. "You did it—you broke the last seal."

Eli wrapped an arm around her, holding her steady. "The path is open now. But what's on the other side . . . "

The gate creaked open slowly, revealing a blinding golden light. Vaughan stepped forward, thinking this was only the beginning of what she was meant to face.

The light beyond the gate was blinding, yet warm. Vaughan stepped through, Eli and Flower close behind. They emerged into a realm unlike anything they had seen before—an endless golden field under a sky where constellations shifted like living things.

At the center stood a throne of crystal, glowing with both light and shadow intertwined. Above it, the crown hovered, radiant and terrifying.

Whispers filled the air, countless voices overlapping:

"She is here."

"The heir has come."

"Will she rise—or fall?"

Vaughan approached slowly. The crown pulsed as if sensing her presence. Each step she took was harder than the last, as if the ground itself was testing her resolve.

Then, the shadows pooled at her feet, rising to form Larzine. He looked battered but not broken, his smile sharper than ever.

"This is where you choose," he said. "Take the crown, and it will either bless you—or consume you. Let me take it, and I will spare you the pain."

"No," Vaughan said, her voice steady. "This is mine."

Larzine sprang forward, and they clashed again, light and shadow spiraling around them. The throne's energy surged, pulling them into its storm. Vaughan's visions erupted one after another: her as a queen ruling with light, her as a tyrant shrouded in darkness, the world burning, the world flourishing.

She realized then—it wasn't just about defeating Larzine. It was about choosing what she would become.

With a cry that tore through the storm, she reached for the crown. The light engulfed her, burning through her veins, blinding her with pain and power.

When the storm cleared, she stood tall, the crown resting on her head, its light pure but edged with shadow. Larzine knelt before her, not by choice, but because the crown's power forced him to.

"You've claimed it," he whispered, his voice filled with both awe and rage. "But light and shadow live within you now. One day, it will eat you alive."

Before Vaughan could respond, he vanished into the darkness, leaving only an echo of his laugh.

The field shimmered and collapsed, and she found herself back with Eli and Flower, the gate closing behind them. The crown's power hummed softly against her skin.

Eli looked at her with a mixture of pride and fear. "You did it. But this . . . this is just the beginning."

Vaughan stared at the horizon where the sky cracked faintly with golden light. She felt both stronger and more uncertain than ever.

In her heart, she knew Larzine was right—light and shadow now warred inside her. And the next battle would not be fought outside, but within.

The crown glimmered faintly under the dim light of Vaughan's bedroom. It didn't glow like it had in the realm beyond the gates. Here, it seemed almost dormant, as if waiting for the right moment to stir again.

Vaughan placed it on the dresser, hesitant to touch it too often. Every time her fingers brushed the cool metal, a surge of energy ran through her veins—sometimes warm and empowering, other times sharp and biting.

She didn't wear it during the day. Something told her not to. Instead, she stored it carefully on the velvet-lined stand Eli had built from scrap wood until they could find something better.

The next morning, she told Eli, "We need to find a case for it. Something safe. Something . . . sealed."

"We can't let anyone touch it. Not even by accident."

They drove to the city, the hum of the engine filling the silence between them. Vaughan stared out the window, watching buildings blur past, her thoughts tangled with both excitement and dread.

Everywhere they went—antique shops, jewelry stores, even specialty boutiques—the crown seemed to hum faintly in her mind. At one shop, the owner, an old man with clouded eyes, froze the moment he saw Vaughan.

"You carry something ancient," he whispered, his gaze fixed on her. "Something that was hidden for centuries."

Vaughan stiffened. "How do you know that?"

The man only smiled, handing her a black case lined with protective symbols. "You'll need this more than you know."

Eli paid without asking questions, but once they were back in the car, he said, "That man knew what you were."

"He knew too much," Vaughan said softly, clutching the case.

That night, she asked Flower the question that had been gnawing at her since the battle. "Why me? Why was this crown hidden from me for so long?"

Flower sighed, sitting across from her with a cup of tea. "Because your bloodline was cursed and blessed at the same time. Long ago, your ancestor—Queen Eliora—sealed away her power to prevent it from falling into the wrong hands. She decreed that only one heir, generations later, would be strong enough to reclaim it. That heir is you."

Vaughan's chest tightened. "And they kept this from me because they thought I couldn't handle it?"

"They kept it because the moment you knew, the shadows would awaken too," Flower said gravely. "And they already have."

At first, Vaughan didn't notice the change. It started with small things: a flicker of anger that burned hotter than usual, a shadow in the mirror that lingered when she moved away, whispers at the edge of her thoughts telling her she was more powerful than anyone else.

When she meditated, she felt two forces inside her—the golden light of the crown and a darker energy coiling beneath it, waiting for an opportunity to take control.

Eli noticed it too. One night, after she snapped at him for no reason, he said quietly, "You're fighting something, aren't you?"

She looked away, ashamed. "It's like part of me . . . wants to let go. To use the power without holding back."

"That's not you," he said firmly. "That's the shadow trying to break free."

Vaughan tried to hold on to pieces of normal life. She spent weekends with Flower, cooking and laughing like they used to before everything changed. She visited family members who didn't know the truth, hiding the crown's existence behind polite smiles.

But even in those moments, the shadow whispered. *They don't understand you. You're above them now.*

She forced herself to ignore it, focusing on mundane routines—

shopping for groceries, walking by the lake with Eli, sipping coffee at quiet cafés. Those moments grounded her, but they were fleeting.

At night, the crown called to her from its case, its energy spilling into her dreams.

~

One evening, she couldn't resist. She placed the crown on her head, just for a moment. The rush of power was intoxicating. Her vision sharpened, and for a second, she felt invincible.

Then the shadow surged, twisting the light into something sharp. She heard Larzine's voice, low and taunting: "You think you control it? You're only feeding me."

Vaughan ripped the crown off, gasping. She shoved it back into the case, locking it tightly.

When Eli found her limp on the floor, he held her without asking questions.

Days turned into weeks. Vaughan tried to resume her routine, attending small family gatherings and helping Flower with garden work. She and Eli went shopping, cooked dinner together, even laughed sometimes.

But the shadow was always there, lurking. Sometimes, when she looked in the mirror, her reflection smiled a fraction too long. Sometimes, when she was angry, objects in the room trembled without her touching them.

The spiritual battle grew more violent. During meditation, she felt herself split—one side radiant and warm, the other cold and commanding. Each side whispered promises.

Light: *You will bring peace.*

Shadow: *You will bring power.*

~

The crown sat inside its case on Vaughan's dresser, sealed, quiet, and yet never truly silent. Even when she wasn't touching it, she felt its pull—a soft vibration in the back of her mind. Sometimes she would wake in the middle of the night and swear she saw faint golden light seeping through the edges of the capsule.

Eli noticed how often she glanced at it when she thought no one was looking. One morning as they had coffee, he said, "You're thinking about it, aren't you?"

"It's like it's . . . calling to me. Not always, but when it does, I feel like I have to listen."

"That's how it works," Eli said, his tone edged with warning. "The crown gives you strength, but it's also testing you. The shadow feeds off your curiosity."

They spent a full day searching for something more secure than the black case the old man had given them. They wandered through hidden markets Eli knew, tucked away behind ordinary streets where rare and strange objects were sold.

In one shop, a woman draped in silk and beads studied Vaughan with an unsettling intensity. "Ah . . . you carry a dual flame," she said. "Light and shadow. That crown is not meant to be contained, only respected."

Eli stepped forward, protective. "We're looking for something to protect it."

The woman nodded and led them to a glass capsule etched with runes that pulsed faintly. "This will hold the crown when you cannot."

When Vaughan touched it, a jolt ran up her arm, as if the capsule recognized her. She bought it without hesitation.

That night, as they secured the crown in its new capsule, Vaughan finally asked Flower directly, "Why didn't anyone ever tell me what I was? I could have prepared."

Flower's eyes softened with sorrow. "Because knowing would have awakened it too soon. The crown doesn't wait—it acts. The moment you became aware of it, the shadow would have stirred. We had to keep you safe until the time was right."

"And the time is right now?" Vaughan asked bitterly.

"Yes," Flower said quietly. "Because now you're strong enough to face it—even if it breaks you first."

Despite the growing tension, Vaughan forced herself to hold on to fragments of a normal life. She visited her cousin's small café, catching up over pastries while hiding the storm inside her. She took walks with Eli, holding his hand while they pretended to be an ordinary couple.

Those moments were grounding, but fleeting. Every laugh, every smile felt fragile, as if one dark thought could shatter it.

Sometimes, she cooked dinner with Eli, and they laughed when they burned the food. Other times, she sat at the table staring at the flame of a candle, watching it bend toward her hand without wind.

It started with whispers in her dreams, but soon the shadow spoke to her when she was awake.

Why do you hold back?

You could destroy anyone who threatens you.

You don't need their help—you're stronger than all of them.

At first, she ignored it. Then she argued with it. But deep down, part of her listened.

One weekend, she spent time with her family. They laughed over old stories, teased her about her stubborn streak, and hugged her goodbye like everything was normal.

But when Vaughan stood in the bathroom that night, looking at her reflection, she saw her smile twist into something cruel—a reflection that didn't belong to her.

They're beneath you, the shadow hissed. *One day, they'll fear you.*

She splashed cold water on her face until the voice faded.

Eli pretended not to notice how often she drifted away during conversations, how her eyes sometimes glowed faintly when she was upset. But he noticed everything.

One night, as they sat on the couch, he said, "You're stronger every day. But I'm afraid of what it's doing to you."

She looked at him, her voice low. "Sometimes I'm afraid too."

Meditation became a battlefield. When she closed her eyes, she no longer found peace—only the blinding clash between golden light and writhing shadow. Her body trembled during sessions, her breaths uneven, as if something inside her wanted to claw its way out.

One night, she saw herself standing between two Vaughan's—one radiant, crowned in pure light, the other cloaked in shadow, her eyes glowing like fire. They spoke in unison: "Choose."

She woke screaming. Eli was there instantly, holding her until the shaking stopped.

After that, the crown began to respond to her moods. When she was calm, it glowed softly. When she was angry, the capsule vibrated, its runes flickering like dying stars.

Flower warned, "The crown mirrors you. If you let the shadow take over, it will follow that path."

Vaughan nodded, but part of her wondered what it would feel like to stop resisting.

Trying to reclaim normalcy, Eli took her out to a quiet restaurant. They laughed, shared a drink. But as they left, Vaughan saw a man watching her from the corner. His eyes glowed faintly—another servant of Larzine.

The shadow inside her surged. *Destroy him.*

She clenched her fists until her nails cut her palms. Eli noticed and pulled her away before she lost control.

Over the next few days, Vaughan felt herself slipping. Her shadow-side grew louder, hungrier, promising power and freedom. The light fought back, burning her from within.

Eli stayed close, but she could see the fear in his eyes—fear not of the enemy, but of losing her to the darkness.

One night, the capsule containing the crown cracked slightly, releasing a faint tendril of black mist. Vaughan stood frozen, staring as the shadow seeped into the air.

She heard Larzine's voice again, soft and taunting: "You can't keep me out forever. I'm already inside you."

Eli rushed to her side, but she waved him back. Her hands glowed gold and black at once as she forced the mist back into the capsule, sealing it with sheer willpower.

When it was done, she felt exhausted.

The next week was deceptively peaceful. Vaughan tried to blend into her routine—morning tea, walks by the lake with Eli, brief visits to Flower where they pretended everything was normal. To anyone else, she looked like a woman rebuilding her life after surviving something extraordinary.

But inside, the shadow whispered louder each day.

When she walked through the grocery store, she caught herself glaring at strangers who brushed too close. When she drove, the shadow hissed at her to take control.

They don't matter. You're the heir. They should move for you.

She clenched the steering wheel tighter, forcing the voice down.

Late one night, as she placed the capsule back on the dresser, she saw a fine crack along one of its runes. The glow inside flickered weakly, as if struggling to contain what was within.

"Eli," she called, her voice tense.

He entered the room quickly. "What happened?"

"The crown—it's pushing against the capsule. It's stronger than the protection."

Eli ran a hand through his hair, pacing. "We need something better. Something ancient. I'll call a contact from the order who—"

Vaughan's eyes narrowed. "Your order? They'll use this as an excuse to take it from me."

Eli hesitated. "I won't let them. You know that."

But she saw the conflict in his eyes.

That night, while Vaughan slept, she dreamed of standing in a blackened field. The moon above dripped red, and at her feet lay the crown—shattered.

Her shadow-self rose from the pieces, smirking. "You're weak. You fight me, but I am you. I can protect us in ways your light never will."

Vaughan backed away. "You're not me."

"Oh, I am," the shadow hissed. "And when they come for us, you'll wish you had let me lead."

When Vaughan awoke, her hands were clenched so tightly her nails had cut her palms.

Three days later, Eli received a coded message. The order knew about the broken capsule. They were coming to "secure" the crown, a term that sounded too much like *take it from her*.

"They're afraid of you, Vaughan," Eli said that evening. "They think if the shadow-side takes over, you'll become unstoppable."

"They're not wrong," she said, her tone sharper than she intended.

Eli stepped closer. "I'm not afraid of you. But they are. And they'll use that fear to justify anything."

Flower came by with herbs and protective charms, her face pale. "I've been having visions," she said. "The order isn't the only danger. The shadow-side inside you is growing stronger. It wants the crown for itself. You must not let it win."

"How do I stop it?" Vaughan asked.

Flower hesitated. "You must face it directly. You can't run from yourself."

Vaughan clung to the semblance of a normal life, hosting a small family dinner to remind herself she was still human. Laughter filled the house, and for a brief moment, she felt grounded.

But as she served food, her vision blurred. Her shadow-self appeared across the table, smirking while the others remained oblivious.

You don't belong here anymore, it whispered. *They would scream if they knew what you've become.*

Vaughan gripped the edge of the table. The voice faded only when she excused herself to the bathroom, trembling.

That night, the shadow-side made its first real move. Vaughan was meditating when the golden light inside her chest flickered and the shadow surged.

Her vision went black, and when it cleared, she was standing in a void where two thrones faced each other—one radiant, one cloaked in darkness. The shadow-self sat on the black throne, smiling.

"Stop resisting," it purred. "I can win every battle for us. Let me."

"No," Vaughan said, her voice steady despite the fear clawing at her. "I won't lose myself to you."

The shadow lunged, merging with her body. Pain exploded through her mind as golden light and black energy clashed.

In the real world, her body shook violently, energy sparking across the room. Eli rushed in, grabbing her shoulders. "Vaughan! Fight it! Don't let it take you!"

With a cry that split the night, Vaughan forced the shadow back, collapsing into Eli's arms, trembling.

The crown pulsed violently inside the cracked capsule, glowing gold and black at once. The runes burned so brightly they nearly disintegrated.

"It's choosing," Flower whispered, eyes wide with fear. "The crown is choosing between the two sides of you."

Vaughan stared at it, tears burning her eyes. "What if it doesn't choose light?"

"Then," Flower said grimly, "you will be the darkness the prophecy warned us about."

For the next few days, Vaughan isolated herself, fearing she might hurt someone. Eli stayed close, refusing to leave her side, while Flower worked tirelessly to reinforce protections around the house.

But the shadow was relentless. It whispered to her when she tried to sleep, it mirrored her movements in the mirror, it urged her to use the crown for power rather than protection.

Sometimes, when she stared at the capsule, she felt the shadow smiling inside it.

The tension built until Vaughan couldn't bear it anymore. One stormy night, she walked out to the lake where the water reflected the fractured sky. Eli followed her but kept his distance.

She stood at the edge, her reflection glowing faintly gold and black. "I can't live like this," she said softly. "I need to end this battle. Now."

Lightning cracked across the sky as she placed the crown on her head, letting its power flood through her. The shadow screamed in triumph, trying to seize control, while the light burned brighter to hold it back.

The storm above mirrored the chaos inside her—lightning and darkness colliding, wind howling.

When Vaughan placed the crown on her head at the lake, the storm above roared louder, as if answering her call. The wind whipped around her, bending the trees, and the water churned violently against the rocks. "Vaughan!" Eli shouted, but his voice was swallowed by the wind.

In an instant, the world shifted. The lake dissolved into darkness streaked with streaks of gold, and Vaughan stood on a battlefield that was both inside her and outside reality. The ground cracked beneath her feet, light pouring through the fissures while shadows rose like smoke from the gaps.

Two forces confronted her: the radiant figure of herself crowned in pure light, and the shadow version, smirking from a throne of obsidian.

"You've come to face me," the shadow said, its voice echoing everywhere. "At last."

8

THE DARKNESS OVERTOOK HER

Vaughan steadied herself, golden energy swirling at her fingertips. "I'm here to end you."

The shadow laughed, cold and smooth. "You can't end me. I am you. I'm the part they all fear. The part they kept chained when they lied to you about who you are."

"They didn't lie—"

"They hid the truth," the shadow interrupted, stepping forward. "You think the crown was made to rule? It was made to control. To force you into a box of light while cutting out the strength of your darkness. They're afraid of what you'd become if you accepted me."

Vaughan's heart raced. "You're lying."

The shadow smiled. "Then why do you feel stronger when you stop resisting me?"

Light and darkness collided, a storm exploding around Vaughan as the two versions of herself lunged at one another. Each strike shook the ground, sending shards of reality into the void.

The light side fought with precision, defending, shielding. The shadow fought with rage, every movement sharper.

"You can't win by hiding from me," the shadow hissed, driving

Vaughan back with a wave of black energy. "You either accept me—or I consume you."

In the real world, Eli knelt beside her body, which floated inches above the ground, glowing faintly gold and black. Lightning cracked across the sky, rain pouring around them.

"Fight it, Vaughan," he whispered, his voice raw. "Come back to me."

The crown on her head pulsed violently, sending ripples of energy that made the earth tremble.

Vaughan gathered herself, standing tall despite the chaos around her. "I won't let you control me."

The shadow tilted its head. "Then use me. You can't win without me."

Golden light surged from Vaughan's chest, clashing with the shadow's dark flames. The two energies wrapped around each other, twisting and exploding, neither yielding.

Visions flashed around them: Vaughan ruling a kingdom bathed in golden light; Vaughan sitting on a throne of bones, her eyes black as night. Both possibilities felt real.

For the first time, the crown itself spoke, its voice deep and resonant: "The heir must be whole. Light without shadow is fragile. Shadow without light is chaos."

Vaughan froze. "Whole?"

The shadow smiled wider. "You see? You don't destroy me—you integrate me."

The battlefield quieted. Vaughan realized the shadow wasn't just an enemy—it was a part of her she had been taught to fear. She stepped forward, placing her hand on the shadow's chest.

"I won't let you control me," she said softly, "but I won't deny you either."

The shadow shuddered, its form merging with hers in a surge of blinding light and darkness intertwined. Energy exploded outward, shaking the void, and when the storm cleared, Vaughan stood alone —stronger, glowing with both gold and black.

The void dissolved, and she collapsed back into her body at the lake. Eli caught her just before she hit the ground, holding her as the storm above faded.

The crown glowed steadily now, no longer cracked or unstable. Its light was golden, but streaked faintly with threads of shadow that pulsed like veins.

Eli stared at it, then at her. "What happened in there?"

Vaughan opened her eyes, her voice hoarse but steady. "I stopped fighting myself. I'm not just light or shadow—I'm both. And that's why I can win."

For the next few days, Vaughan rested, her body healing from the spiritual battle. The shadow no longer whispered with malice; instead, it spoke with quiet strength, a voice that reminded her of the power she carried when she balanced both halves of herself.

Flower visited and gasped when she saw Vaughan's new energy. "You've done what no heir before you has. You've embraced both sides."

"What does that mean?" Vaughan asked.

Flower smiled faintly. "It means the prophecy has changed. And so has your destiny."

Life returned to a fragile calm. Vaughan spent time with family again, feeling more grounded than before. She and Eli shared quiet evenings, sitting by the fireplace, speaking little but feeling everything.

The crown stayed in its capsule most of the time, but now when

Vaughan touched it, it didn't fight her—it pulsed gently. Yet she knew this peace wouldn't last.

One night, as she slept, she dreamed of Larzine. He stood in a burning field, his cloak torn, but his eyes still glowed with defiance.

"You think you've won," he said. "But every time you use that crown, I'll be there. Waiting. Watching. Growing."

When Vaughan woke, the crown hummed faintly, as if it too had heard him.

In the days following the battle within herself, Vaughan carried a new presence. People noticed it—even strangers. When she walked into a room, heads turned, though most didn't understand why. She didn't have to say anything; she commanded attention without effort.

Eli noticed the change most. He watched her quietly, as if he were memorizing this new version of her. "You're different," he said one evening.

Vaughan gave a small smile. "I'm whole."

But with the light and shadow balanced inside her, her power had also become unpredictable. At times, when her emotions surged, the ground beneath her feet vibrated faintly, or objects trembled without touch.

She was stronger than ever—but also walking a razor's edge.

Vaughan tried to keep her life as normal as possible. She spent time with Flower, who had softened noticeably since the prophecy shifted. They cooked together, shared tea, and spoke about mundane things.

But even Flower's laughter was edged with tension. She watched Vaughan closely, as if making sure her daughter's light truly outweighed her shadow.

Family gatherings were both comforting and haunting. Vaughan loved being with her relatives, listening to their stories, yet part of her felt like an outsider now. When she looked at them, she kept hearing the shadow's calm voice: *They have no idea who you are. They could never understand what you've become.*

She ignored it, but the voice lingered.

Despite the progress she had made, the crown remained an almost living entity in its capsule. Sometimes at night, she'd hear it hum, a low vibration that matched her heartbeat.

One morning, she opened the capsule just to check on it. The crown pulsed faintly, threads of gold and black swirling like smoke. She touched it briefly, and a surge of warmth and cold spread through her veins at the same time.

She quickly closed the capsule, her breath shaky. "Not yet," she whispered to herself.

Meanwhile, Eli's order had grown restless. They no longer sent warnings—they sent spies. Vaughan felt eyes on her when she walked through town, and sometimes she spotted figures in the distance who vanished when she looked twice.

Eli confronted his contacts one night, his voice low and dangerous. "She's under my protection. If you come for her, you'll go through me first."

The contact sneered. "She's not your responsibility anymore. She's a threat to everything."

When Eli returned, his face was grim. "They're preparing to move against us. It's only a matter of time."

One rare afternoon, Vaughan and Eli took a break from the tension. They went to a small coastal town, walking along the beach with coffee in hand. For hours, it felt almost like a date—light conversation, soft laughter, the ocean breeze cutting through the heaviness in their lives.

Eli teased her about her overpacked bag. She teased him about his stubbornness.

But as they sat watching the sunset, Vaughan's vision blurred. The golden sky turned black, and she saw Larzine standing in the waves, his eyes burning.

"Enjoy your peace while it lasts." His voice echoed inside her head. "Because what comes next will make you wish for me instead."

When she blinked, the vision was gone—but the dread remained.

Her shadow-self had changed since the integration. It no longer hissed with malice but offered warnings and insights.

The order is not your only enemy now, it said one night as she meditated. *Something older stirs in the dark. Something even Larzine fears.*

Vaughan's pulse quickened. *What is it?*

The voice didn't answer.

That same night, the sky outside the townhouse rippled unnaturally, as if reality itself was bending. A low hum filled the air, vibrating through the walls.

Flower stormed in, her face pale. "Do you feel that? This isn't the order. This is something else."

Eli grabbed his weapon instinctively. "What now?"

Before anyone could respond, the hum stopped. The silence that followed was worse than the noise.

Vaughan stared at the window. "Something's coming."

In the following days, Vaughan tried to hold her normal life together. She went shopping with Flower, spent quiet evenings reading, and sat on the porch with Eli, watching the stars.

But every night, the crown pulsed louder. Every day, the order's presence crept closer. And every vision Vaughan had was more cryptic, filled with images of something massive and ancient moving just out of sight.

One evening, Vaughan was brushing her hair when she froze. Her reflection in the mirror smirked at her, though she hadn't moved her lips.

"You think you've tamed the darkness," the reflection said in a voice that wasn't hers. "But you've only opened the door."

The glass cracked. She stumbled back, and Eli rushed into the room, grabbing her shoulders. "What happened?"

"The mirror spoke." Vaughan's voice shook.

Flower pored over the ancient book night and day, finally revealing a hidden page that had appeared under moonlight.

"The prophecy mentions something called 'the Devourer,'" she said, trembling. "It's older than the crown, older than the bloodline. It awakens when light and shadow merge in one vessel."

Vaughan's stomach dropped. "Me."

Flower nodded. "You're the vessel. And it's coming for you."

That night, Vaughan was pulled into another vision. She stood in a black void, the air thick like tar. From the darkness, a massive shape emerged—something that was not human, not even shadow. Its voice was like thousands of whispers.

"Little queen," it said. "You have what I need. When I take it, nothing will stop me."

Vaughan tried to summon light, but the creature's presence snuffed it out. She woke gasping, her body drenched in sweat.

Eli held her, whispering, "You're safe."

But she wasn't.

The next morning, the crown in its capsule flared violently, threads of black and gold twisting like a storm. The capsule nearly cracked open.

Vaughan stared at it, fear and determination mingling in her chest. "It knows."

Before she could process the vision, the order made its move. Eli sensed them before they arrived, grabbing Vaughan's hand. "They're here."

Masked figures surrounded the house, their weapons glowing faintly. They weren't there to negotiate—they were there to take the crown.

The shadow within Vaughan stirred. *Let me help you.*

For the first time, she let the shadow flow with the light, her energy flaring as she stepped outside.

The battle was quick and brutal. The order's soldiers were skilled, but they weren't prepared for Vaughan's merged power. With every wave of her hand, golden-black energy erupted, disarming them and sending them sprawling.

Eli fought alongside her, moving with deadly precision.

When it was over, the order retreated, leaving behind only their warning: "We'll be back. And next time, we won't fail."

The house was silent again, but the silence felt heavy. The crown pulsed faintly, and Vaughan knew the order wasn't their only problem anymore.

She sat with Eli and Flower by the fire, the three of them speaking quietly, knowing this was only the beginning of something much worse.

The shadow's voice returned, low but steady: *The Devourer is coming. Prepare yourself.*

The days following the order's failed attack were unsettlingly quiet. Vaughan's power grew rapidly, almost as if it was feeding on the conflict. Sometimes the lights in the house flickered when she walked by. When she concentrated, she could bend small streams of energy in her hands like liquid.

But her nightmares about the Devourer became stronger. She'd wake up with her heart pounding, drenched in sweat, sometimes with the taste of ash in her mouth.

Eli tried to keep her grounded, training with her every morning. Yet even he noticed that her energy was becoming harder to control. "You're stronger," he said one day, breathing heavily after sparring. "But it's wild."

"I can feel it," Vaughan said, clutching her side. "The Devourer's influence. It's not just outside—it's inside me."

As night fell, the house creaked in unnatural ways. Shadows stretched too far across the walls, twisting into strange shapes. Flower scattered salt and burned herbs in every room, whispering protective incantations.

"It's probing," Flower said one evening, her face pale. "It's testing the barriers we've put up."

Vaughan stood by the window, watching the moonlight ripple unnaturally. "It's not testing. It's learning."

The order's messages to Eli became more aggressive. One night, while Vaughan slept, his communicator buzzed. The voice on the other end was cold: "You've had your chance to deliver the crown. You've failed. If you stay with her, you will die with her when the Devourer comes."

Eli's jaw tightened. "Then I'll die with her."

"You're a fool," the voice hissed. "You could have been spared."

When he hung up, he stared at Vaughan as she slept. He brushed a strand of hair from her face, whispering, "I'm not leaving you."

Flower worked tirelessly through the night, poring over the ancient book. The pages revealed something she hadn't seen before —a ritual older than the seals themselves.

"This can protect you," she told Vaughan, "but it's dangerous. It requires a tether—someone willing to bind themselves to you completely."

Vaughan glanced at Eli, who said without hesitation, "I'll do it."

Flower frowned. "You don't even know what it costs."

"I don't care," Eli said firmly. "I'm not letting her fight this alone."

The ritual required rare elements—herbs that burned blue, a circle carved with runes, and the crown placed at its center. Flower prepared everything meticulously, her hands trembling as she worked.

Vaughan sat cross-legged in the circle, Eli kneeling opposite her. "Are you sure about this?" she asked softly.

"Completely." He locked eyes with her.

As Flower chanted, the runes glowed faintly, and the crown

pulsed violently. Energy surged around them, threads of gold and black weaving through the room.

Eli reached out, taking Vaughan's hands. Their connection flared, and the energy wrapped around them both.

Then a voice—deeper than anything they had heard—rumbled through the house:

"You think you can protect her from me?"

The Devourer's presence filled the room like a suffocating fog. The candles flickered wildly, their flames bending toward the crown.

Through the swirling energy, the Devourer spoke again, its voice like an echo from a void.

"She is mine. The crown chose her because she carries both light and shadow. When she falls, I will rise through her."

Vaughan gritted her teeth. "You won't have me."

"You already feel me," the voice hissed. "And soon, you'll call to me."

The ritual continued, Flower's chanting growing louder. The energy tightened, forming a barrier that pushed the Devourer back—but only temporarily.

When the light finally dimmed, Vaughan collapsed against Eli. The crown stopped pulsing violently and settled, but faint black veins still streaked across it.

For a day, peace returned. Vaughan spent time with Eli, sitting on the porch as the sun set, sipping tea, speaking softly about everything but the battles ahead.

But that night, she dreamed again.

She stood in a ruined city under a sky torn open by shadow. Buildings crumbled into dust, and rivers of black fire ran through the streets. At the center stood the Devourer, a colossal shape with no defined form—only shifting darkness and eyes like burning stars.

It spoke without moving: "Every time you use the crown, you feed me. Every victory brings me closer. You can't win."

Vaughan raised her hands, summoning light and shadow, but the energy was swallowed instantly.

When she woke, she was shaking. Eli held her, whispering, "You're here. You're safe."

But she knew safety was an illusion.

The next day, the sky over the town darkened unnaturally at noon. Animals fled, and the wind carried whispers in a language no one understood.

Flower clutched her chest. "It's breaching the veil. It's coming through."

The crown pulsed so violently that the capsule cracked again, shards of energy leaking into the air. Vaughan grabbed it, feeling the surge burn through her veins.

Eli stepped forward. "Vaughan, don't—"

But she held on. "I have to. It's calling me."

That night, the Devourer manifested partially in the physical world. The sky split open above the lake, pouring black fire that hissed on contact with the water. The creature rose from the rift, massive and formless, its voice shaking the earth.

"You can't hide from me, heir. You are my doorway."

Vaughan stepped forward, her eyes glowing gold and black. "Vaughan!" Eli shouted, but she raised a hand to stop him.

"You want me?" she said, her voice steady. "Then come and take me."

The Devourer roared, the sound cracking the air, and lunged.

The night air burned as the Devourer rose higher from the black rift. Its shape shifted endlessly—sometimes resembling a towering humanoid figure, other times a storm of writhing tendrils. The lake boiled beneath it, sending up clouds of steam. The ground quaked, trees bent, and the air itself screamed.

Vaughan's heart pounded, but she stood firm. The crown on her head glowed fiercely, threads of gold and black swirling together like a storm. Eli stood behind her with his weapon ready, even though he knew no blade could harm this thing.

The Devourer's voice shattered the silence: "You dare to stand against me, vessel?"

Vaughan's jaw tightened. "I'm not your vessel. I'm your end."

A massive wave of shadow shot from the Devourer's form, crashing toward her like a tidal wave. Vaughan raised both hands, summoning a dome of golden-black energy. The impact shook the earth, but she held her ground.

The shield cracked under the pressure, forcing her to release an explosive pulse of energy that lit up the night. The wave of light forced the creature back, and for a moment, the rift flickered.

Eli shouted, "You're hurting it! Keep going!"

But Vaughan felt her strength draining fast. Every use of her power pulled at something deep inside her, something she couldn't afford to lose.

The Devourer reared back, its voice thundering: "Do you know why the crown exists? It wasn't forged to save you. It was forged to bind me. You are its last prison."

The revelation hit her like a blow. "What?"

"Every heir is a lock. Every heir is sacrificed to keep me chained. You are the final lock, and when you break, I will be free."

The shadow's words from earlier whispered back in her mind: *They made the crown to control you.*

Eli's voice cut through her thoughts. "Vaughan, don't listen to it! It's trying to break you!"

But doubt clawed at her chest.

Explosions of light burst from the forest. Figures from the order emerged, weapons glowing, chanting in unison. They weren't there to help—they were there to seal Vaughan away with the Devourer if they had to.

Their leader shouted, "Contain the heir! Do not let her bond with it!"

Eli stepped in front of them, blade drawn. "You're not touching her!"

The order soldiers spread out, their weapons forming a net of energy. Flower appeared on the ridge, shouting protective spells that slowed them down.

Vaughan's energy faltered under the combined chaos.

Inside her, the shadow-side stirred violently. *You're losing. Let me take over. Let me fight.*

Vaughan gritted her teeth. "No. I'm not giving in."

You can't win without me.

She hesitated for a heartbeat too long. The Devourer struck again, a tendril wrapping around her waist, lifting her off the ground. Pain burned through her body as it tried to pull her into the rift.

"Vaughan!" Eli screamed, charging forward, slicing at the tendril with his blade. The strike barely cut through, but it gave her enough time to release a burst of energy, freeing herself.

Breathing hard, Vaughan rose slowly, her eyes glowing with both light and darkness. "You want a vessel? Then you'll have to take all of me."

She stopped fighting her shadow-side and instead pulled it into her light, merging them fully. Her energy flared, a storm of gold and black so bright it made the soldiers shield their eyes. The Devourer recoiled, its form trembling.

Flower shouted from the ridge, "She's doing it! She's becoming whole!"

Energy erupted from her body, clashing with the Devourer's darkness. The sky split with lightning, the rift widened, and the earth cracked.

The Devourer roared in pain as parts of its form disintegrated under her power. But every attack she landed drained her faster. Blood ran from her nose, her breaths came ragged, but she didn't stop.

The creature's voice roared in fury: "You will break before I do!"

She screamed back, "Not today!" and sent a final surge of energy into the rift.

The rift collapsed, pulling the Devourer back into itself. But the pull caught Vaughan too, dragging her toward the darkness.

Eli ran toward her, grabbing her hand. "Hold on!"

She looked into his eyes and whispered, "If I go, seal it behind me."

"No! I'm not letting you—"

"Promise me!" she cried, tears mixing with the rain.

The Devourer's tendrils wrapped around her legs, pulling harder. Eli held on with everything he had. Flower screamed from the ridge, chanting desperately.

In a last burst of power, Vaughan released her hold on the physical world, letting the Devourer drag her into the rift—but as she went, she forced her energy into the crown.

The crown exploded in a flash of light, sealing the rift as it closed.

The rain stopped, and the soldiers retreated, their leader muttering, "She's gone. The seal holds—for now."

Eli fell to his knees where she had been, clutching the cracked crown. Flower ran down to him, tears streaming.

"She's not gone," Eli said hoarsely. "She's inside the crown. I can feel her."

The crown pulsed faintly in his hands, threads of gold and black swirling slowly.

For Vaughan, there was no pain—only silence. When the rift closed, she found herself standing in an endless expanse of shimmering gold streaked with black veins. It was beautiful and terrible, like walking inside the heart of the crown itself.

She touched the air, and it rippled like water. Each step echoed, not outward, but inward, as if the space was alive.

"You've trapped yourself here," a voice whispered.

She turned and saw the Devourer—smaller now, a coiled mass of darkness, still bound but not destroyed. Its eyes glimmered with hate.

"You sealed the gate, but you sealed yourself with me."

Vaughan clenched her fists. "Then I'll keep you here forever."

The Devourer's laughter was low, resonant. "You think eternity will not change you? The shadow in you is mine. I will wait."

The crown's realm bent time. Vaughan didn't know if days or weeks passed, but she wandered through landscapes shaped by her own memories: her childhood home, the lake, the battlefield where she faced Larzine. Each place whispered secrets—some comforting, some threatening.

At times, she heard Eli's voice faintly, as if through a wall: *Hold on, Vaughan. I'm coming for you.*

The Devourer taunted her constantly, twisting its form into shapes she feared, feeding on her doubts. But she also discovered something: here, her power was limitless. The realm responded to her will.

And she would use that to keep the Devourer caged.

Outside, Eli kept the crown close at all times. He slept with it on the nightstand, his hand resting on it as if that could reach her. He talked to it, not caring if Flower thought he was losing his mind.

"She's in there," he said one night, staring at the faint glow. "I know she is."

Flower worked tirelessly on spells and rituals, her hands raw from endless sigil carving. "I've found something," she said finally. "A way to bridge to her. But it's dangerous—if we fail, we could lose her forever."

Eli's voice hardened. "Then we don't fail."

9

THE CROWN'S POWER

The order didn't intervene directly, but Eli knew they were still watching. He could feel their eyes when he left the house, shadowy figures lurking at the edge of his vision.

They were waiting—either for Vaughan to return or for the crown to fall into their hands.

"They're just biding time," Flower warned. "If we succeed, they'll see her as a threat all over again."

"Then let them try," Eli muttered.

Using Flower's ritual, they created a circle of runes around the capsule holding the crown. Blue flames burned at its edges, and Eli knelt inside the circle, his hands on the capsule.

"Focus on her," Flower said. "Call to her spirit. The bond you share may be enough to guide her back."

Eli closed his eyes and spoke softly. "Vaughan, if you can hear me—fight. I'm here. I'm not letting you go."

The crown pulsed in response, its glow intensifying. A faint golden-black thread stretched between him and the crown.

In the crown's realm, Vaughan paused. A thread of light appeared before her, cutting through the darkness. She felt Eli's voice ripple through it like a heartbeat.

The Devourer hissed. "Do not follow it. You belong here with me."

Vaughan gripped the thread, feeling strength surge through her. "No. I belong with them."

The darkness rose to block her, but she unleashed a wave of energy, forcing it back. The golden-black thread pulled her forward, brighter and brighter until it consumed everything.

In the physical world, the crown exploded in light. The capsule shattered, and Eli shielded his eyes.

When the light faded, Vaughan knelt in the center of the circle, breathing hard, her skin glowing faintly with threads of gold and shadow.

Eli dropped to his knees, pulling her into his arms. "You're back."

She leaned against him, whispering, "You called me."

"You came," he said, holding her tighter.

When Vaughan stood, the glow around her dimmed, but she felt different—heavier, stronger, and not entirely human anymore. The Devourer's voice was still faint in her mind, no longer taunting but waiting.

We are not finished.

She clenched her fists. *No. But I'm ready for you.*

Days later, Eli spotted an order envoy waiting outside their home. The man spoke with calm menace: "She's changed. She's no longer what she was. If she loses control, we will intervene."

Eli stepped forward, his voice sharp. "You'll have to go through me first."

The envoy smirked. "We expected nothing less."

That night, Vaughan stared at the crown—now cracked but glowing with a deeper, darker light. Her reflection in the glass of the window smirked faintly, her shadow-self speaking softly:

You think this was the end? The Devourer isn't the only thing waiting. The real war hasn't started yet.

As the wind howled, Flower joined her on the porch. "You're not the same, Vaughan."

"I know."

"Whatever's coming, it's bigger than anything we've seen."

Vaughan looked out into the night, the faint glow of the crown reflecting in her eyes. "Then we'll be ready."

Far above, the stars flickered unnaturally.

The days following Vaughan's return were strangely calm. She moved through life as if she were learning to live in her own skin again.

Eli stayed close to her, a constant anchor. He cooked for her, trained with her, and silently watched her when she thought he wasn't looking. Flower kept herself busy strengthening protective wards around the house.

Vaughan knew the stillness was only temporary—like the moment before a storm breaks.

Her power had changed. Even mundane tasks—turning on a light, pouring water—seemed to hum with energy beneath her fingertips. She found herself avoiding mirrors, where her reflection sometimes moved a heartbeat out of sync.

One evening, she asked Eli quietly, "Do you see it? That I'm . . . different?"

He looked at her for a long moment. "Yes. But you're still you."

She wanted to believe that.

The order grew bolder in their surveillance. Drones hummed overhead at night, cloaked figures appeared at the edges of town, and she could feel eyes following her every time she stepped outside.

Flower slammed a book shut one afternoon. "They're not going to wait forever. They're building a case to justify taking you by force."

Eli's jaw tightened. "Let them try."

But Vaughan knew the order wouldn't come with half measures—they'd bring everything they had.

That night, Vaughan dreamed of chains—glowing ones, wrapped around her arms and throat. In the dream, the order's leader stood over her, chanting as the chains tightened, draining her power.

She struggled, but the chains bit deeper, glowing brighter.

A voice whispered from the darkness: "They'll use your own light to bind you. And when they do, I'll be the one to set you free."

She woke trembling, the shadow inside her stirring restlessly.

The crown pulsed violently the next morning, sending a low hum through the house that rattled the windows. Vaughan stood before it, hand hovering over the cracked surface.

"Something's coming," she murmured.

Eli stepped beside her, his weapon already in hand. "Then we'll face it."

Three nights later, as they prepared for another day of training, a figure appeared at the edge of their property. It wasn't the order.

It was Larzine.

Vaughan tensed, summoning energy to her hands, but he raised them in mock surrender. "Relax, heir. I didn't come to fight."

"Then why are you here?" she demanded.

"To warn you," he said smoothly. "The Devourer isn't your only problem. The order is preparing a weapon designed to strip you of the crown and burn out your power completely."

Eli growled, stepping forward. "Why should we believe you?"

Larzine smirked. "Because I want you alive. If anyone is going to destroy you, it will be me—not them."

According to Larzine, the order had crafted something called the *Scepter of Severance*—a relic capable of cutting the bond between Vaughan and the crown. Once severed, she'd be powerless, and the Devourer would rise unchallenged.

"They're planning to use it soon," Larzine said. "I suggest you prepare."

Vaughan studied him, suspicious. "Why warn me at all?"

His smile was faint and dangerous. "Because I'd rather face you at full strength."

With that, he vanished into shadow.

Knowing the order was preparing a direct assault, Vaughan pushed herself harder than ever. Eli trained with her until both of them were exhausted, his body bruised, her energy unstable but growing more precise.

She practiced summoning both light and shadow at once, learning to weave them instead of letting them clash. The power felt natural now, like an extension of her.

But with every success, the shadow whispered: *You're still feeding me. You're still feeding the Devourer.*

Flower uncovered another hidden page in the prophecy, one that made her blood run cold.

"It says," she told Vaughan, "that the heir will face three trials: one within herself, one against the Devourer, and one against the world. You've passed the first two. The third . . . is about to begin."

"What is it?" Vaughan asked.

"It doesn't say," Flower replied grimly. "Only that the heir must 'burn to rise anew.'"

By the end of the week, the air around their home shimmered faintly with energy—an unmistakable sign that the order had set wards.

"They're closing in," Eli muttered.

"They're not here yet," Flower said, "but they will be soon. We have little time."

Vaughan stood with her arms crossed, the crown's glow reflecting in her eyes. "Then let them come."

That night, as she drifted into sleep, her shadow-self appeared beside her, calm but serious.

"They're not your only enemy anymore," it said. "There's something older watching all of this. When the order strikes, it will strike too."

Vaughan frowned. "Older than the Devourer?"

"Yes," the shadow said simply. "And it's already moving."

The night before the order was expected to attack, the house was silent. Flower meditated in her room, Eli cleaned his weapon in the living room, and Vaughan sat on the porch, staring at the stars.

Eli sat down beside her quietly. "You're thinking about the fight?"

"I'm thinking about what comes after," she said softly. "If I survive this, what's left of me?"

He reached over, taking her hand. "Whatever happens, you'll still be you."

She leaned against him, drawing strength from his presence.

Just before dawn, the wards around the house flared. A cold wind swept through the property, carrying the scent of metal and ozone.

"They're here," Flower said, stepping onto the porch with a burning sigil in hand.

Figures from the order emerged from the trees, cloaked in silver light, weapons glowing. At the center, their leader carried the Scepter of Severance.

Vaughan stepped forward, the crown pulsing on her head. The light and shadow around her swirled violently, forming a storm that shook the ground.

The leader raised the scepter. "By decree of the order, you are to be stripped of your power and contained. You are too dangerous to exist."

Vaughan's voice was calm but sharp. "Then you'll have to kill me to do it."

The soldiers moved, the leader charged, and the sky itself cracked open as the third trial began.

Far above, something ancient stirred in the stars, watching with hunger.

Dawn split the horizon with a pale light, but it was swallowed quickly by the storm forming above Vaughan's home. Clouds swirled unnaturally, lightning crawling like veins across the sky. The order stood in perfect formation, their silver weapons reflecting the eerie light. At the center, their leader gripped the Scepter of Severance—a weapon humming with an energy that made even the air tremble.

Vaughan stepped forward, the crown pulsing in sync with her heartbeat. Light and shadow swirled around her, forming a vortex that bent the grass beneath her feet.

Eli stood at her side, blade drawn. "Stay close to me."

Flower raised her protective sigil high, chanting under her breath. "The wards won't hold long against that scepter. Be ready."

The leader raised the Scepter of Severance, and a beam of pure white energy shot toward Vaughan. She countered instinctively, throwing up a shield of gold and black. The beam struck the shield, sending a shockwave through the ground, knocking soldiers and trees alike off balance.

The order pressed forward, weapons glowing as they surrounded her. Their chant filled the air, creating an oppressive rhythm that made Vaughan's energy flicker.

She unleashed a pulse of power, sending several soldiers flying. But the leader advanced unfazed, swinging the scepter in arcs that tore holes in her protective barriers.

"You can't win," he said coldly. "The scepter was forged to unmake the crown's bond."

As soldiers closed in, Eli became a blur of movement, cutting through their ranks. His weapon clashed with theirs, sparks flying in every direction. He moved to protect Vaughan at every angle, taking hits meant for her.

"Keep fighting!" he shouted, blocking another strike. "You can do this!"

Flower dropped to her knees, drawing symbols in the dirt with trembling hands. The sigils burned blue as she chanted an incantation older than the order itself. A barrier rose around them, slowing the soldiers but draining Flower's strength rapidly.

"Vaughan!" she cried out. "You need to end this before they break the circle!"

Before Vaughan could strike, the sky cracked open with a sound like shattering glass. The stars above seemed to twist, bending into a spiral. A massive shape emerged from the tear in the sky—not the Devourer, but something older, something far more terrifying.

10

ENTITY ATTACHMENTS

The entity descended, its form shifting between fire and void. The order froze in terror.

Even the leader faltered, lowering the scepter slightly. "No . . . it can't be awake."

The entity's voice was a thousand whispers layered into one: "The crown's heir burns brightly . . . and so does the feast."

Vaughan felt the entity's gaze pierce through her. The shadow inside her stirred violently, warning her: *This is the real enemy. Older than me. Older than the Devourer. It wants everything.*

The entity reached toward her, and the Scepter of Severance pulsed in response. The order scattered, their chants breaking into chaos.

Eli shouted, "Vaughan! What is that?"

Her voice was steady despite the fear in her chest. "The third trial."

The crown's energy flared, burning with blinding gold streaked with threads of darkness. Vaughan drew power from both sides of herself, the merged light and shadow roaring to life. She stepped forward, her body glowing like a living star.

The ancient entity hissed, the sound making the ground splinter.

It lashed out with tendrils of void-fire, but Vaughan caught them in her hands, burning them away with her energy.

"This ends here," she said, her voice resonating with power.

The entity and Vaughan collided in a storm of energy that ripped the sky open. The order fled to the tree line, shielding their eyes from the blinding light. Eli held his ground, shouting, "Vaughan!" as the shockwaves tore through the earth.

Every strike from the entity was met with Vaughan's power. Her light burned holes through its void while her shadow countered its fire. The battle felt endless, each blow shaking the world itself.

The entity roared: "You burn, but fire consumes!"

Vaughan screamed, "Then let it consume everything that threatens this world!"

She summoned every drop of her power, pulling the energy of the crown into herself. Gold and black flames erupted from her, spiraling upward into the sky. The entity shrieked as the flames tore through its form, shattering it.

The explosion that followed was blinding. For a moment, the world was nothing but light.

When the light faded, the entity was gone. The sky cleared, and the stars shone normally again. The order's leader knelt on the ground, stunned, the Scepter of Severance dimmed and useless.

Vaughan stood at the center of the scorched earth, the crown on her head glowing faintly, cracks running across its surface like veins of fire. Her body trembled, but she remained standing.

Eli rushed to her side, catching her before she collapsed. "You did it," he said, his voice breaking.

Flower stumbled toward them, tears streaking her face. "The prophecy was true . . . she burned to rise anew."

The leader of the order stood slowly, his eyes fixed on Vaughan. "You are beyond our control. For now, we withdraw. But know this— we will be watching."

He and his soldiers vanished into the night, leaving only the smell of burned earth behind.

As Vaughan rested in Eli's arms, the shadow inside her spoke one final time, calm but ominous:

You've won this battle. But the fire inside you burns hotter with every victory. One day, it may burn you too.

She closed her eyes, whispering, "Then I'll burn brighter than anything that dares to come for me."

Far above, in the silent void beyond the stars, something stirred—a presence even the ancient entity had feared. It watched the earth quietly, waiting.

Vaughan recovered slowly in the following days, her power stable but more intense than ever. She spent her time with Eli and Flower, cherishing the quiet moments, even as she felt the weight of what was coming next.

The crown now hummed with a deeper resonance, as if holding secrets it had yet to reveal. Vaughan stood on the porch one night, staring at the stars.

"The real war hasn't even started," she murmured.

Eli wrapped an arm around her shoulders. "Then we'll face it together."

She smiled faintly, her eyes glowing gold and black. "Together."

The house was too quiet. Even after the battle's scars were cleared, the air retained a metallic taste of power. Vaughan woke often, pacing through the halls, her bare feet cold on the floorboards.

Every shadow seemed to stretch when she looked at it too long. She told herself it was nothing, but the crown—locked in its capsule—continued to hum at night.

When she finally fell asleep, her dreams were fractured: flashes of the ancient entity's disintegrating body, tendrils of void-fire wrapping around her legs, and whispers in a language older than time.

She woke with a start, drenched in sweat, to find Eli sitting in a chair by her bed, watching her.

"You were screaming," he said softly.

Vaughan rubbed her temples. "It's never quiet in my head anymore."

He leaned forward, gripping her hand. "Then let me share the noise."

For the first time in days, she smiled.

The days blurred together, but they weren't peaceful. The Devourer's voice was gone, yet Vaughan felt a darker presence creeping in at the edges of her senses.

The shadows in corners seemed to shiver when she passed. The air grew cold when she lost her temper, and sometimes objects cracked just from her touch.

"You're . . . changing again," Flower said quietly one morning while Vaughan brewed tea.

"I know." Vaughan stirred the cup slowly. "It's not the Devourer. It's something worse."

Eli refused to let the fear swallow them whole. One night, he lit candles and cooked dinner—simple, grounding, human. They ate quietly, exchanging small smiles.

Later, as the storm raged outside, Vaughan found him on the couch, reading. The lace of her thin white nightgown glowed in the candlelight as she walked toward him.

Eli's eyes softened. "You should be resting."

She sat beside him, close enough that their shoulders brushed. "I can't sleep."

He leaned in, brushing his lips against hers, a kiss that deepened slowly. When he pulled back, he rested his forehead against hers. "Whatever's coming, we face it together."

She whispered, "I'm afraid of what I'll become."

"I'm not," he said firmly.

The next night, Vaughan dreamed of an endless black ocean where voices cried out from beneath the waves. Something moved below, a shape so enormous it distorted the water.

When it surfaced, she saw not one creature, but many—eyes glowing faintly, mouths opening in silent screams. The water turned to blood, and hands reached out, grabbing her ankles.

She woke up choking, the taste of salt and ash in her mouth.

The crown pulsed violently in its capsule, and cracks spidered along its surface again.

Flower burst into her room at dawn, clutching the prophecy book. "It's here. The presence I warned you about—it's not just watching anymore. It's sending something ahead of it."

"What?" Vaughan asked, her voice hoarse.

"A harbinger," Flower said. "A creature that will prepare the way for it. If it reaches you, it will mark you."

Outside, the sky darkened unnaturally, and the wind carried a sound that was not quite a scream and not quite a whisper—something inhuman.

Eli grabbed his weapons. "We're not letting it near her."

Then the harbinger came. It wasn't like the Devourer—it wore tattered robes as it walked through the woods, with its face hidden, its steps silent. The ground withered where it walked.

Vaughan felt it before she saw it. Her power surged wildly, and the crown in its capsule rattled violently.

The figure stopped at the edge of the property, its voice dry and hollow: "The stars have sent me to claim the heir. Hand her over, and I will be merciful."

Eli stepped in front of Vaughan, blade drawn. "Over my dead body."

The figure tilted its head, almost amused. "So be it."

The storm above broke with violent rain as the harbinger

attacked. Its movements were unnatural, flickering like static. Every strike it made cracked the ground, sending waves of void-fire.

Eli fought fiercely, but the creature was relentless. Flower's spells slowed it, but not enough. Vaughan stepped forward, the crown glowing on her head despite the risk.

Her merged power flared, light and shadow spiraling into a blade of energy in her hand. She clashed with the harbinger, each strike tearing pieces of the storm apart.

The creature laughed, its voice a hundred whispers: "You're only feeding the one that sent me."

With a scream, Vaughan struck through the harbinger's chest. The creature let out a sound like shattering glass as it disintegrated into black ash, carried away by the wind.

For a moment, the storm calmed. But the victory felt hollow.

Where the harbinger fell, a single burning sigil remained on the ground. It pulsed faintly, showing images in the air: a massive shape in the stars, its tendrils wrapped around planets, its eyes like suns.

The voice of the ancient presence boomed through the night: "Little heir . . . I am coming."

The sigil exploded, and the wind died.

Back inside, Vaughan collapsed into Eli's arms. Her skin burned, veins glowing gold and black. Flower knelt beside them, whispering prayers.

"She's marked," Flower said. "The harbinger touched her. Whatever sent it now has a path to her."

Eli held Vaughan close. "Then we fight it before it reaches her."

That night, Vaughan and Eli clung to each other. They made love slowly, as if to remind themselves that they were still more than the forces trying to claim them.

Afterward, Eli traced a finger along her shoulder. "You're the strongest person I've ever known."

She whispered, "Stay with me. No matter what I become."

"Always."

Two nights after the harbinger's destruction, the stars above the town dimmed as though swallowed by a creeping shadow. Vaughan stood on the porch, barefoot, wrapped in a blanket, staring upward. The constellations shifted unnaturally, twisting into unrecognizable shapes.

One constellation split open like a wound, oozing faint streaks of black light that dripped into the sky. A voice—not loud, but impossibly vast—whispered into her bones: "You are my wound. You are the tear I will crawl through."

Eli stepped behind her, wrapping his arms around her shoulders. "You're trembling."

"The sky is bleeding," she said, her voice hollow.

He looked up and saw only stars. But he didn't argue.

The next day, Flower returned from gathering supplies with a pale face. "They're here," she said.

"Who?" Vaughan asked.

"They don't call themselves anything," Flower replied. "No name, no symbol. They don't believe in worship—they believe in *alignment*. They think the thing in the sky is the true shape of the universe. They see you as the 'key that will finish the pattern.'"

Eli frowned. "Pattern?"

"They believe reality is broken," Flower said. "To them, the crown is the missing piece to heal it. They want you not to destroy the entity —but to let it through."

Vaughan's stomach tightened. "They think I should open the door."

"Yes," Flower said grimly. "And they'll do anything to make that happen."

They came at night. Not as an army, not as zealots shouting, but as individuals—men and women who looked like ordinary townsfolk. They carried no banners, wore no robes, spoke no chants. They stood silently at the edge of the property, their heads tilted upward as if listening to something Vaughan couldn't hear.

When she stepped outside, one of them—an older woman with sunken eyes—spoke softly:

"You're the seam. We only ask that you stop resisting."

Vaughan's skin crawled. "And if I don't?"

The woman's smile was empty. "Then you will suffer until you do."

Without another word, they turned and walked back into the night, vanishing like mist.

For the next few days, birds flew in spirals until they dropped. Mirrors fogged without heat. Random people in town stood still for hours, whispering under their breath.

One morning, Vaughan woke to find symbols carved into the trees around the property—perfect circles intersecting with sharp lines, patterns that made her dizzy to look at.

Eli burned them, but new ones appeared the next night.

"They're mapping the door," Flower said, voice trembling. "And they're using you as the center."

The cult—if it could be called that—didn't attack physically. Instead, they turned reality against her. She'd open a door and find herself standing in a hallway that stretched into endless darkness. She'd blink and see blood dripping from the walls, only to vanish a second later.

Sometimes she'd see them inside the house, standing silently in corners, their faces blank. When she blinked, they were gone.

The crown pulsed more violently at night.

Eli stayed close, his hand always on her back, his eyes scanning every shadow.

One night, after hours of tension, Vaughan found herself sitting on the kitchen floor, knees pulled to her chest. Eli knelt beside her, brushing hair from her face.

"I'm not strong enough," she whispered.

"You are."

"You don't see it—sometimes I *want* to give in. It would be easier to stop fighting."

Eli cupped her face, forcing her to meet his eyes. "Then I'll fight for you until you remember who you are."

She kissed him, desperate and trembling, and they wound up in each other's arms. It wasn't passion born of lust—it was survival, a reminder they were still human.

Later that night, she dreamed of standing on a glass bridge suspended in space. The cult members walked beneath it like shadows, tracing patterns on the stars.

The entity's voice rumbled through her head: "They draw my shape. When the pattern is complete, I will arrive."

The glass cracked beneath her feet. She woke screaming, and the crown pulsed so violently it shattered its capsule entirely.

The next evening, dozens of them stood around the property, forming a perfect circle, their bodies swaying slightly in unison. Their mouths moved, but no sound came out.

The sky above split again, the bleeding constellation expanding. As the ground vibrated, Vaughan clutched the crown, feeling its heat burn her hands.

Flower shouted, "They're opening a doorway! If they finish the pattern, we're done!"

Eli charged into the circle, cutting through the silent figures, but they simply crumbled into ash when struck. More appeared from the trees—their movements jerky, unnatural.

Vaughan placed the crown on her head, her energy exploding

outward. The cult faltered, their pattern breaking as golden-black flames tore through the night.

The sky screamed.

The voice of the ancient entity roared through the sky, shaking the ground: "You can't stop what is written!"

Vaughan screamed, "Then I'll rewrite it!"

She unleashed her power in a spiral of light and shadow, burning through the cult's lines, breaking their alignment. The stars above snapped back to their normal positions, and the wound in the sky closed.

The surviving cultists dissolved into mist, leaving only the echo of their whisper: "We will try again. Until the pattern is complete."

Vaughan fell to her knees, the crown humming faintly, its cracks glowing like molten veins. Eli caught her, holding her tightly.

"You stopped them." His voice shook.

"For now," she whispered. "But they'll keep coming."

Flower stepped closer, her face pale. "That wasn't the real war. That was just the first move."

That night, Vaughan looked at the stars again. They looked normal, but she could feel it—the presence beyond them, waiting. Watching.

It whispered softly, almost tenderly: "You burn beautifully, little heir. I'll come for you soon."

The days following the cult's failed alignment were filled with an unnatural stillness. It wasn't peace—more like the breath a predator takes before it pounces.

At night, Vaughan would stand on the porch with Eli, staring at the stars. The constellations no longer bled, but they shifted subtly, like eyes blinking in slow motion. When she turned away, she felt them watching.

One evening, she whispered, "They're not done. The stars— they're moving closer."

Eli tightened his grip on her hand. "Then we keep fighting. Whatever comes, we face it."

The cult returned, but this time they weren't human at all. The ones who had dissolved into mist had left pieces of themselves behind, which formed shadowlike dark fragments that stretched unnaturally. Their faces were featureless except for faintly glowing lines where eyes should have been. They moved silently, appearing at the edge of Vaughan's vision, vanishing when she blinked.

Flower burned herbs at every window, her hands shaking. "These are not people anymore. They've let the entity reshape them. They're ... its messengers now."

Eli sharpened his blade. "Then we cut down the message."

That night, Vaughan dreamed she stood in a room filled with mirrors. Each reflection showed her in a different form: crowned in light, crowned in shadow, crowned in fire. Some of the reflections whispered: "Break the crown and be free."

Others hissed: "Break yourself and let us through."

Then the mirrors cracked, and black fluid poured out, rising to her chest. From it, a massive eye opened, staring into her soul.

"You are not the heir. You are the doorway."

She woke gasping, clutching the crown.

The following evening, she sat in the living room with Eli, the storm outside casting shadows across their faces. She leaned against him, whispering, "If I'm just a doorway, what am I fighting for?"

He pulled her closer. "For the choice to stay yourself."

She looked at him, her eyes shining with tears. "You're the only thing keeping me human."

They kissed deeply, clinging to each other as the world fell apart. Their love burned against the cold creeping in from the stars.

The next night, as she touched the crown, it spoke in the form of thoughts that poured into her mind.

You were made to hold me. I was made to bind the stars. Together, we keep the sky from collapsing.

Vaughan's breath hitched. "Who made you?"

The crown pulsed, showing her flashes: an ancient civilization, beings of light forging the crown from a dying star to seal away something monstrous. They sacrificed themselves to embed the crown's power into their bloodline—her bloodline.

The vision ended with a whisper: *You are the last flame. If you go out, the sky burns.*

～

The next time the cult appeared, they infiltrated the town. People Vaughan knew began acting strangely, their voices too smooth, their movements too precise. Some spoke to her in riddles:

"The pattern is almost drawn."

"The stars hunger for your crown."

"Stop resisting, and you'll finally see."

The most horrifying moment came when a child approached her, his eyes glowing faintly. He handed her a folded piece of paper before vanishing.

Inside was a perfect drawing of the sky, with the constellations shaped into an open mouth.

That night, Eli insisted they leave the house for a while. They drove to a secluded cliff overlooking the ocean, the moonlight spilling across the waves. For a few precious hours, they laughed, kissed, and lay under the stars, pretending they weren't being hunted.

"You're everything to me," Eli whispered against her neck.

"And you to me," she said breathily.

The moment was soft, intimate. But deep inside, Vaughan felt the stars watching, their silence mocking the fragile beauty of what they had.

～

The cult attacked the next night as a single entity. Their bodies merged, forming a horrific mass of flesh and shadow that towered over the trees. It moved like a spider, its limbs cracking unnaturally.

Its voice was dozens of voices layered together: "Open. Open. Open."

The ground split where it stepped, and the smell of burning metal filled the air.

Eli grabbed Vaughan's hand. "Inside! Now!"

But Vaughan didn't move. She placed the crown on her head, her power flaring. "No. This ends now."

The creature lunged, its many mouths screaming silently. Vaughan unleashed golden-black energy, blasting chunks off its body, but it regenerated instantly.

Flower hurled protective charms, buying moments of time. Eli fought at her side, cutting at the limbs, his movements fueled by fury.

The creature wrapped tendrils around Vaughan, pulling her toward its core. Her vision blurred as it whispered: "Give in. Let the stars feed."

Her shadow surged, merging with her light, and she screamed, releasing a shockwave that shattered the creature into burning ash.

When it died, the sky above shifted violently, forming a spiral that glowed faintly with red light.

Flower clutched her chest. "Every time we destroy one, it opens the way a little more."

Vaughan stared at the sky. "Then next time, it won't send pieces of itself. It'll come itself."

That night, she and Eli held each other in silence. They didn't speak of the battles, only of small things—childhood memories, dreams of a life far away from all of this. They made love with the desperation of those who feared there would be no tomorrow.

When they fell asleep, Vaughan whispered, "If I fall, don't let me become their doorway."

Eli kissed her forehead. "I'll burn the sky before I let that happen."

At dawn, a shadow passed over the house, blotting out the sun for a moment. A massive eye opened briefly in the clouds, looking directly at Vaughan.

The entity's voice slid into her mind, gentle and terrifying: "I'm almost there."

The morning began like any other, but Vaughan felt it before she saw it. A vibration thrummed through the ground, through the air, through her bones. When she looked up, the sky fractured.

The crack spread across the clouds, glowing faintly with red light, like molten veins beneath glass. Birds scattered in chaotic patterns, screaming as they fled.

Flower ran out to the porch, clutching her spellbook. "It's happening faster than I thought."

Eli's hand gripped his weapon, though he knew it was useless against the sky. "What's causing this?"

Vaughan stared upward, her voice barely above a whisper. "It's trying to break the veil."

The cracks widened at night, and fragments slipped through. Shadows that slithered along the ground, whispering her name. Fingers of light that burned whatever they touched. Faces appearing in reflections, screaming silently before melting away.

One night, while brushing her hair, Vaughan saw her reflection smile at her. *You can't stop it*, it whispered. *You'll only make it hungrier.*

She smashed the mirror, her breath ragged.

The order came at dawn—this time not as enemies, but as survivors. Their leader stepped forward, his silver cloak torn, his expression grim.

"The cracks aren't just here," he said. "They're everywhere. Cities are vanishing. Entire forests collapsing into void."

Eli moved to stand protectively between him and Vaughan. "Why are you here?"

The leader's voice was tight. "To form an alliance. If this thing comes through, it won't care who wins or loses. It will devour everything."

Vaughan studied him with cold eyes. "And what's the catch?"

He hesitated. "The crown. We'll need to use its full power, even if it destroys you."

Eli snarled, "That's not happening."

The order proposed a ritual—a massive working of combined power to slow the cracks. Flower studied their plans and confirmed its effectiveness, but her voice trembled when she said, "It will drain Vaughan. Possibly kill her."

11

BATTLE OF THE HEIRESS

Vaughan said nothing for a long moment, then nodded. "I'll do it."

Eli grabbed her arm. "No. You've given enough."

She met his gaze, her eyes glowing faintly. "If I don't, the world ends. This isn't about me anymore."

That night, before the ritual, Eli pulled her into his arms and kissed her like it was the last time. "If you die, I'll follow you. Don't ask me not to."

She cupped his face, tears in her eyes. "Then fight with me. Don't let them turn me into their weapon."

The order gathered around a massive circle carved into the ground, glowing with runes that pulsed like a heartbeat. The cracks above widened, stars flickering like dying embers.

Vaughan stepped into the center, the crown on her head, light and shadow swirling around her. Flower stood at the edge, chanting protection spells. Eli stood ready, blade in hand, watching her with unblinking intensity.

As the ritual began, energy surged through Vaughan's veins, burning her from the inside. The sky screamed, the cracks widening faster.

The entity's voice rolled across the land: "You cannot stop me, heir. You can only feed me."

The more power Vaughan channeled, the more the cracks pulsed with light, revealing glimpses of what lay beyond: landscapes of flesh and fire, oceans of eyes, towering beings kneeling before an even greater shape.

Her nose bled, her vision blurred, but she forced more power into the ritual.

The order's leader shouted, "Enough! You'll kill yourself!"

Vaughan screamed, "I'm not stopping!"

Eli rushed forward, grabbing her arm, grounding her just enough that she didn't collapse. "Come back to me. Don't let it take you."

A tendril of void-fire reached through one of the cracks, wrapping around Vaughan's waist. The ritual faltered as the sky bled darker, the energy turning chaotic.

The entity's voice was almost tender now: "Stop fighting, little heir. I'll make it painless if you open the door."

For a moment, she felt herself weakening, tempted by the promise of an end to the pain.

Eli's voice cut through the fog. "Vaughan! You're stronger than it. Remember who you are."

With a cry that tore her throat raw, she burned the tendril to ash.

The cracks screamed, sealing partially. The stars shifted back into their proper positions, but the wound still remained—a jagged line glowing faintly in the night.

The entity's voice receded, but not with defeat. "You've only delayed me. When I come, there will be no sky left to save."

Vaughan clung to Eli, her hands shaking. The order watched in silence, awe and fear in their eyes.

The leader spoke softly, almost reverently. "She's not just the heir. She's the fire that holds back the dark."

Eli glared at him. "And she's not yours to use."

They left quietly, knowing this alliance wouldn't last.

For two days, the world was still. Vaughan rested, Eli never leaving her side. Flower worked on new wards, her face drawn with exhaustion.

But Vaughan knew it wasn't over. In her dreams, she saw the stars bleeding again, the cult reforming in stranger shapes, the entity's true form stretching across galaxies.

Each night, the voice came closer, whispering: "Soon, little heir. Soon."

~

It began on the third night after the ritual, when the stars no longer moved naturally. They didn't twinkle—they *stared*, tracking Vaughan as she walked the perimeter of the property.

The crown, resting against her chest, throbbed with heat. It whispered in pulses, rhythms that felt like warnings.

Eli joined her outside, his expression tense. "You feel it too, don't you?"

She nodded, her voice low. "It's not hiding anymore. It's already here—just not in a form we understand."

The wind shifted unnaturally, carrying an ashen smell. When they looked toward the horizon, a plume of gray smoke rose. It was *dust* drifting like snow. Each flake shimmered faintly, and when one landed on Vaughan's arm, it burned like acid.

She slapped it off, trembling. "This isn't ash. It's alive."

~

By dawn, the sky was thick with gray. The sun struggled to break through, casting the world in a dim, sickly light. Townsfolk whispered of nightmares where they woke with ash in their lungs, their skin peeling into gray powder.

Flower burst into the room, her eyes wide. "This isn't weather. It's a precursor. Something massive is hiding in that ash."

When Vaughan looked out the window, she saw a colossal shadow moving behind the haze, its outline shifting like smoke but with a clear shape—an *eye*, closing and opening as it drifted over the earth.

The eye blinked, and the ground beneath their feet trembled.

The cult returned, but this time they were unrecognizable. Their bodies were thin, almost skeletal, covered in the same ash that burned the air. Their eyes glowed faintly red. All Vaughan heard was the wind howling through hollow spaces.

They simply stood in rows, tilting their heads at impossible angles, waiting.

Eli tightened his grip on his blade. "They're not even human anymore."

Vaughan stepped forward, the crown pulsing on her head. "They're not here to worship. They're here to summon."

The ash above thickened, the shape within growing clearer. The eye blinked again, and this time a voice, alien and vast, filled the air.

"Little heir . . . you burned my messenger, and you shattered my harbinger. Do you think the sky will hold against me?"

Vaughan shouted, "You're not crossing through!"

The voice chuckled, deep and resonant. "I already have."

From the ash, something slithered down—an arm that wasn't an arm, jointed wrong, covered in shifting eyes. It touched the ground, and the earth turned to black glass where it rested.

The cult fell to their knees, their bodies cracking open as more ash poured from their mouths, forming new shapes.

Eli stepped in front of Vaughan. "Stay behind me."

But she pushed past him. "This is my fight."

The arm lashed forward, faster than anything she'd seen. Vaughan barely raised a shield in time, the impact sending her flying backward into Eli's arms. The ground where she had stood dissolved into liquid shadow.

Her power surged, both light and darkness spiraling out of her hands. She hurled a beam of energy at the arm, burning through it—but instead of retreating, it *grew*, splitting into two new appendages.

Flower shouted over the chaos, "It's feeding on your attacks!"

The voice slid into Vaughan's mind, soft and intimate: "Why fight me when you can be me? You've already merged light and shadow. Merge with me, and you'll become everything."

For a moment, she felt herself waver. The power it offered felt intoxicating—limitless, all-consuming.

Eli grabbed her shoulders, shaking her. "Don't listen! Vaughan, stay with me!"

His voice grounded her. She tightened her grip on the crown and screamed, "I'm not yours!"

The appendages lashed again, aiming for Vaughan. Eli threw himself in front of her, his blade glowing as he intercepted the blow. The impact shattered the weapon and sent him flying, his body crashing into the ground.

"No!" Vaughan screamed, rushing to him.

He coughed, blood on his lips. "I'm fine . . . just—just fight."

Her shadow-self surged violently, fueled by rage.

The crown's cracks widened, bleeding black light. Vaughan felt something inside her snap—her humanity trembling on the edge of collapse. She let the shadow pour through her, weaving it with the light until her energy became something entirely new: golden fire laced with dark streaks that moved like liquid.

The cult screamed—not with voices, but with their bodies splitting open as they burned from the light pouring off her. The arm recoiled, shrinking back toward the ash cloud.

The eye above narrowed.

"You've tasted it now. The forbidden fire. Every time you use it, you burn yourself."

As she pushed her power higher, Vaughan realized something horrifying: the cracks in the sky weren't the doorway at all. They were distractions.

The true door was inside her—her merged nature, her bloodline, her very being. The entity wasn't trying to break through the veil; it was trying to break *her*.

Flower screamed, "It's not coming through the sky—it's coming through you!"

Vaughan drew all her power into a single point, focusing not on destroying the entity, but on sealing herself from it. The flames around her turned black and gold, twisting into a storm that swallowed the ash, burned the cult, and forced the eye to close.

The sky cleared abruptly, the cracks fading, the world returning to silence.

She collapsed next to Eli, who groaned but pulled her close. "You ... you did it."

"For now," she whispered, her voice hoarse.

The order arrived too late to help, watching from the tree line with awe and fear. Their leader muttered, "She's not human anymore."

Vaughan turned her head toward him, her eyes glowing faintly. "You're right. I'm not."

He flinched.

That night, Eli held her as they sat on the porch, the stars above looking deceptively calm. She rested her head on his chest.

"They'll keep coming," she said softly.

"Then we keep fighting."

She closed her eyes, whispering, "Promise me you won't leave."

"Never," he said, kissing her hair.

Far above, beyond even the stars, something opened its eyes—a presence so vast it made the previous horrors seem small.

The voice slid into her dreams that night, colder than ever: "You've delayed me twice. But every time you burn, you burn away pieces of yourself. When you're hollow, I will step through."

12

SHE'S GONE

She woke with the taste of frost on her tongue.

For a jagged instant, Vaughan didn't know where she was—only the echo of that voice, unspooling like black thread through the corridors of her mind. Then the scent of smoke and old paper steadied her. The sanctuary's great hall had burned itself down to embers. Orange light licked the arches, painting the night in ribs of shadow.

Sunshine slept on the floor beside her, hand still wrapped around hers as if the slightest looseness would invite the darkness back. Flower had curled against the base of the broken statue, one arm slung over her eyes. Eli stood watch by the shattered rose window.

"Bad?" Eli asked without turning.

"Not as bad as it thinks," Vaughan said, though her pulse hitched.

Eli finally faced her. His eyes were the color of tarnished coins, steady and old. "The Hollowing takes little bites first. It wants you to notice the missing pieces."

Vaughan pulled herself up. Her joints ached in that precise way they had after every burn—magic flaring through her veins, leaving ash where it had been. "I noticed."

Sunshine stirred, lashes trembling. He didn't release her hand. "Tell me."

She told them what she could remember: the cold, the voice, the promise of stepping through when she was empty. Flower listened without interruption, but the way her jaw set said she was composing her own promise back. Sunshine's thumb moved against Vaughan's pulse, counting it like a rosary.

"It speaks like a magistrate," Flower muttered finally. "All verdict, no blood."

Eli's mouth slid wryly to one side. "It prefers bargains, actually. You'll hear the offers soon. Not tonight. It isn't stupid enough to come while the ward-embers are still warm."

"The wards are barely there," Sunshine said. He glanced up at the ribs of glass and star. "And we can't sleep out here again."

Eli nodded. "Come. I'll show you where to lay your heads until dawn. The rooms were sealed before the siege. Stone and salt. Even a hungry thing remembers its manners around salt."

He led them down a side passage Vaughan hadn't noticed earlier, a narrow door hidden behind a tapestry of woven sea-grass. They descended a tight spiral, boots whispering against limestone. The air cooled as they went, pulling the heat from their skin until Vaughan's breath fogged faintly. Her magic quieted too, the burn receding to a blue ember in the bone.

At the base of the steps, the corridor opened into a cloister of cells arranged around a small courtyard. No sky showed above—only a skylight of old glass glazed with night. The rooms themselves were monk-simple: a bed with a thick wool blanket, a carved chest with a sprig of rosemary tied to its handle, a hooked shelf bearing a chipped basin, and a bar of soap the color of bees. On each windowsill: a line of salt as neat as a stitch. Vaughan touched it and felt, beneath her fingertip, a low hum like a cat's purr.

"Apprentices used to stay here," Eli said, pushing open doors one by one. "Before the Order decided to pretend the dark was extinct."

"They pretended?" Flower asked.

"Extinction is tidier than vigilance," Eli said. "And it makes better speeches."

Sunshine snorted without humor. "We're past speeches."

He chose the room at the far corner where the wall met the curve of the corridor—two stone angles to brace against. Flower took the cell across from him, fingers lingering on the rosemary until the sharp scent threaded the air. Vaughan stepped into the last room and felt something in her chest loosen.

It wasn't safety. She doubted that existed anymore. But it was an arrangement of small, human comforts that said: This is how people live while the world tilts.

Eli lingered at her threshold. "You want the lamp or the dark?"

"Leave the lamp," Vaughan said. "If it comes back, I want to see it coming."

He took a stub of chalk from his pocket and drew a sigil over the door, lines intersecting like a compass. "For true names," he said. "In case it tries to wear someone else's."

"Will it?"

"It learns quickly," Eli said. "So must you."

Vaughan's throat felt full. "If I burn again—"

"You will," Eli said, not unkindly.

"Then I may not be myself," she finished. "Pull me back if I don't know you."

"I will," he said. "And if I can't, Sunshine will. And if he can't, Flower will drag you by that fierce hair and remind you that you made her a promise."

Vaughan exhaled, a ragged laugh catching on something like a sob. "Good night, Eli."

"Say rather: Night," he said. "Good, we'll craft ourselves."

He moved on, drawing sigils, straightening blankets, making the ancient look briefly inhabited. Sunshine kissed Vaughan's forehead in the doorway. "I'll hear you if you call."

"I know," she said. He left, soft steps fading. Flower poked her head in, eyes enormous in the lamplight, and squeezed Vaughan's fingers once. Then the corridor quieted, and Vaughan lay down.

Sleep came in loops: a slip-knot of images, the voice tugging them tight. She floated through the hall of embers. She walked the night orchard where the fruit hung too high and bled shadows when she pierced their skins. She crossed the bridge of glass. And there it was: the presence, distantly patient, the void with an iris.

"You built your fire as a wall," it said. "You will learn that a wall is just a circle waiting for a door."

"What do you want?" she asked, exhausted.

"Entry," it said. "And quiet. Your world is so loud. All that beating."

"Go to the sea," Vaughan said. "That's loud too. Maybe it will drown you."

The laugh unrolled like smoke. "The sea empties into me. I am the mouth that waits beneath all mouths. But I am polite. Stop burning, and I will be patient. Burn, and I will hurry."

Vaughan woke again, heart lurching, lamp guttering. The chalk sigil above the door gleamed faintly. Her skin itched as if ash clung to it. For one panicked instant, she tried to remember a song her grandmother used to sing—something about a ship and three stars—but the words were cut up and scattered, blank edges where there should have been a tune.

A piece, she thought, sitting up. That's a piece missing.

She swung her legs over the side of the bed and touched the floor. Cold stone. The salt line was undisturbed. The door sigil intact. She listened, really listened, to the corridor. Somewhere a pipe creaked like an old man turning over in his sleep. Somewhere else, a page flipped.

Sunshine snored very softly when he was truly spent; she didn't hear it. Worry spidered out from her sternum.

Vaughan stood and opened her door.

The corridor was bruised with shadow, the lamps turned down low. Vaughan padded to Sunshine's cell and looked in. The bed was empty but rumpled, the blanket dragged like a tide had pulled at it. His satchel lay open, journal half out, pen uncapped. No blood. No struggle's scatter. Only absence, which was worse.

"Eli?" she whispered, but he was nowhere visible. Flower's door was ajar. Inside, Flower slept curled like a comma, one hand fisted around the rosemary sprig, hair making a dark fan on the pillow. Vaughan felt her impulse to wake Flower rise and fall. No—let her have one hour, two.

She turned back toward the stairs. Something flickered at the edge of her vision like a moth. She reached out—and her hand sank through the light as if into water. It wasn't a moth. It was a memory the Hollowing had loosened from its hook and set to drift.

Sunshine, laughing, chalk dust on his nose. Sunshine, teaching her to strip wire gingerly. Sunshine, the scar along his shoulder from a night she hadn't been there—no, from a night she had been there and had closed the door behind her to hold a circle that would have collapsed if she'd left. But the details wobbled like heat above asphalt. She pressed two fingers hard to her temple. "No," she said to the air. "You don't get him."

"Then keep him," the voice breathed near her ear, impossible. "Find him. Burn for him. Show me where your door is."

She didn't run. She wanted to. Instead Vaughan moved through the quiet like a blade. Down the corridor. Up the coil of stone stairs. Through the sea-grass tapestry back into the ruined hall where the embers jittered and died. The rose window at the far end wore the night like a bruise.

"Sunshine?" she called, and her voice didn't carry; it slid into the stone and stuck there.

Eli stepped from the shadow of the altar. He looked older in the ember light, as if the night had sanded his edges. "I hoped you'd sleep."

"Sunshine's gone."

Eli didn't startle. "He isn't gone," he said. "He's above."

"Above what?"

Eli tipped his head. "Come."

They crossed the hall and shouldered a half-collapsed door that groaned in complaint. Beyond it, a narrow stairwell angled upward, ladder-steep, the stone worn concave by centuries of feet. The air smelled different here—damp, metallic. Vaughan's hand trailed the wall and came away wet.

"The north tower," Eli said softly. "We kept the astrarium up here. It used to show the turning of the sky. The Order dismantled it when they decided not to be superstitious. Occasionally, superstition saves your life."

"Is Sunshine with an antique?" Vaughan asked.

"With the sky," Eli said.

At the top, the stairwell resolved into a circular room with a domed ceiling skin-pricked with embedded mica. The astrarium was a carcass of brass ribs and glass bands, pieces removed, cogs stacked like coasters. And in the middle of it all, on the ledge of the broken oculus, Sunshine sat with his legs dangling into the void, face turned up to the small square of night.

Vaughan's lungs remembered how to work and promptly forgot, because he was humming—the same cut-up song she'd been trying to recall. The words were gone, but the shape of them remained. She crossed to him, fury and relief braided so tightly she could scarcely distinguish them.

"You absolute idiot," she said.

He looked over and smiled in that lopsided way. "Couldn't sleep," he said. "Everything down there is too tight. Up here it feels like a lid lifted."

She stood next to him at the oculus, hands flat on the crumbling stone. The sky beyond was a black lake. Stars pricked it. Far above, something moved—no, it didn't move. It was the movement of every-thing else around a center like an eye.

"You heard it too," Sunshine said.

"Yes."

He tapped the brass with one finger. It sang a low, soft tone. "I think it's trying to make you burn again. I think it needs you to. The burns punch pinholes. It wants enough holes to pour itself through."

"Then I won't burn," Vaughan said, flinching at the lie. Her magic had never felt like choice; it had taken her choices and wrapped them in heat until they made sense.

Sunshine considered her. "You will," he said gently. "But maybe not the way it expects."

She swallowed. "I came to drag you back to bed."

"Bed's a story we tell our bones," he said. "Here's another: Once, a girl looked up and decided to make the sky smaller. Not by cutting it, but by naming it. Not everything that looks at you gets to keep its gaze."

He held out a hand. On his palm lay a shard of glass as thin as a fingernail, etched with a circle crossed by a single line—the simplest of the old signs. "Found it under the gear-teeth. If you don't burn, anchor. Hold a line."

Vaughan closed her fingers around the shard. It was cool, and the etching was shallow, and yet a weight gathered behind the sign.

"Do we wake Flower?" Sunshine asked.

"In a minute," Vaughan said. "Tell me the song."

He hummed again. She matched him, note for note, the melody filling its own missing pieces. When she misremembered, Sunshine didn't correct her; he adjusted, and the song accommodated the lie until it became a truth that fit the night. Eli sat at the ruined astrarium's edge and added a lower thread, old and steady.

When the last note thinned into the stone, the presence above them paused. Vaughan felt it—just a sliver of hesitation. She lifted the glass to the oculus and drew the horizon sign in the air, the etching aligning with a seam in the sky. It didn't close—she hadn't expected miracles—but it narrowed very slightly.

Pain flashed in her forearms. She looked down. Fine black lines threaded her skin where fire had traveled before, but instead of burning, they were cooling, ink settling. Not emptiness—definition. The voice didn't speak. It waited.

"Back to the rooms," Eli said softly. "Dawn will make us fools if we greet it with our mouths hanging open."

They returned the way they'd come. In the corridor, Flower stood in her doorway, hair wild, rosemary clenched in her fist like a weapon. "If either of you vanish without a note again," she said, "I will burn the whole place down and sift you from the ash."

Sunshine looked properly chastened. "Noted."

Vaughan showed her the glass. Flower's expression altered, annoyance and awe making a temporary truce. "That's old craft," she said. "Older than the Order. My grandmother had one in her sewing kit. Said a straight line was another kind of spell."

"Keep it," Vaughan said, pressing the shard into Flower's palm. "If I forget the words again, sing to me."

Flower's fingers closed around the sliver. "Promise me you won't leave."

"Never," Vaughan said, and this time when she said it, it wasn't a desperate vow to the uncaring darkness. It was to the three of them, and to the straight line they would hold together, through whatever came.

They slept then, not because they were safe, but because even hunted things must rest. Vaughan's dream returned, but the voice stayed at a distance, irritated by the music, troubled by the horizon. It tried to whisper hollow; she breathed full. It tried to pry; she laced her fingers, felt other hands lace with hers.

When dawn finally found them—thin pale light pooling along the corridor floor—Eli was already up, chalking a larger compass on the hall's stone, muttering to the lines as if they were stubborn, beloved animals. Flower brewed tea that smelled like mint and thunder. Sunshine stood at the rose window, face tilted to the day as if he could siphon courage from light.

Vaughan joined them, the ash-taste gone from her tongue. Far above, the presence hung like a bruise you could almost forget until you breathed too deeply. It would come again. It would test, bargain, threaten, and wait for the burn.

"Let it wait," she said.

"Let it starve," Flower said, fierce as morning.

Sunshine smiled, and this time, there was no tremor to it. "And if it doesn't?"

Vaughan flexed her hands. "Then we give it something it didn't ask for." She looked at the horizon they had drawn together and felt, for the first time, the shape of another door—one that opened out, not in.

"Breakfast first," Eli said dryly. "Then heresy." He set the chalk down and straightened, the compass complete. "You can change a world on an empty stomach, but it tends to make you unkind."

They laughed because the alternative was to count the cracks in the ceiling until the fear fell through. They ate. And when the bowls were empty and the tea was gone, they made a list on the back of Sunshine's journal—a list of the names they would gather, the old crafts they would steal back, the songs they would learn.

Far above, something watched.

Far below, four names wrote themselves in chalk and salt and breath and refused to be erased.

The dawn was thin and stingy. They finished the list on Sunshine's journal in cramped handwriting and underlined the last line twice:

Doors that open outward.

"First step?" Flower asked, blowing across her tea until the steam wrote secrets on the air.

"The astrarium," Eli said. He tapped his chalk-dusted fingers together. "If we can reset even a sliver of its measure, we can mark where the sky bruises most. That's where the door will try to form. We plant our line there."

Sunshine bent over the brass ribs like a clockmaker coaxing a sleeping thing awake. "Half the cogs are missing, and the other half are sulking."

Vaughan touched the curved spine of the machine. It thrummed faintly at her palm, as if remembering the discipline of being useful. "What do you need?"

"Teeth," Sunshine said. "We need teeth. And oil. And three lengths of ribbon. Don't look at me like that. Ribbons are practical magic. Everyone who knew what they were doing tied things with ribbon."

"Kitchen," Flower said, vanishing down the stairs, her steps a rush of intent. She returned with a tin of oil, a jar of old screws whose heads looked chewed, and a roll of red silk ribbon more at home around a gift than a machine. Vaughan felt the small domesticity of it click against the night's vastness.

They worked. Eli chalked arcs on the floor, muttering measures under his breath. Sunshine fitted cogs until the ribs engaged with a grudging click. Flower tied ribbon in clever knots. And Vaughan sang —not the whole song, just the intervals that steadied her breath and kept the lines on her arms cool.

When her voice slipped, Sunshine hummed her back into place. When Sunshine's fingers shook, Flower's ribbon bound his wrist. When Flower's temper flared, Eli looked at her with that old, coin-dark steadiness and said, "Yes," as if he were agreeing with her anger before it had to bite someone to be believed.

By the time the pale daylight found its courage, the astrarium stirred. The glass bands rattled, then settled. A brass pointer shivered, then swung slowly, as if cautious. It settled on north-northwest. The mica in the domed ceiling caught the light and flung it across their faces in small, glittering wreckage.

"That way," Sunshine said. The pointer quivered again like a dog straining its leash. "It doesn't like being watched."

"Nothing hungry does," Eli said. He wiped his hands on a rag and tucked the chalk behind his ear. "We can follow the bruise and find where it thickens. If the door's forming, we can head it off."

"Before it forms, or as it forms?" Flower asked.

"Yes," Eli said, and Vaughan decided not to forgive him for that answer yet.

They packed: oil and ribbon, a coil of wire, a knife with a handle worn smooth by other frightened hands, the rosemary sprig now tied in Flower's hair like a warrior's joke. Sunshine took his journal, and after the smallest hesitation, tore their list out and tucked it into Vaughan's coat pocket. "It belongs next to your heat," he said softly. "Not in my bag where the dark can paw through it."

They left the sanctuary by the west door, the one with the stone saints whose faces had been weathered into blankness. The city woke around them by degrees. Old glass caught light. Street cats considered them like judges and then dismissed them. A woman in a green coat watered a window box and wished them a good morning like a blessing or a dare. Vaughan breathed in bread and coal and river and felt, briefly, the shape of a life that paused for market days and contained nothing with an iris.

They turned north-northwest, following the feel of the bruise the way you follow the memory of a name. The streets thinned to warehouses and rust-scabbed rails. Beyond, the cranes stood like patient herons. The river was a wide, gray muscle. The pointer circle Sunshine had sketched on a bit of card tugged his hand toward a ferry dock that had not seen a ferry in a decade.

Eli stopped at the edge of the water. He crouched, dipped two fingers into the river, and drew a wet line across the dock's rotting planks. "Horizon," he said.

Vaughan felt the sign like a ridge beneath her foot. The bruise in the sky concentrated here, a pressure she could feel in her teeth. She swallowed against it. Sunshine flanked her. Flower shifted her weight, trying not to look like someone bracing against a blow.

"It wants you to burn," Sunshine whispered, not accusing, not pleading, just saying.

"I know," Vaughan said. "So we do something else."

Eli's gaze flicked to her arm where the inked lines lay like cooled rivers. "Tell me."

"I open," she said, surprising herself with the clarity of it. "But not in. Out."

"The other door," Flower breathed. "Outward, not inward."

"Can you?" Eli asked, not doubting, not encouraging. Measuring.

Vaughan closed her eyes and reached the way she had reached on the tower—toward the space where naming made the sky smaller. She held the hum of the sign under her foot, the weight of the list in her pocket, the shape of Sunshine's hand when it had closed over hers in the night. She did not reach for heat. She reached for line. For edge. For the place where choices happened.

She felt the world consider her. The bruise bent. The river's surface stilled.

"Now," she said through her teeth. "Sing."

Sunshine's hum threaded the air. Flower joined, her voice lower, rougher, but Eli didn't sing. He spoke, a litany of measures like directions to a place you've never been but believe in because someone you trust says it is there.

Vaughan opened.

Not heat. Not the wild sprawl of fire, but a hinge, a gasp of pressure equalizing as if someone had opened a window in a room you hadn't realized was stale. The bruise tore like fabric separating along a seam that had been waiting to part.

Beyond it, not darkness. Not yet. Wind poured through, smelling like salt and cold iron and the inside of a stone.

It was working. She felt it: The door was not an invitation to step in, but a path for something to leave—the way a house coughs smoke when a chimney is unblocked.

"Hold," Eli said, voice steady. "Hold."

Flower's fingers dug into Vaughan's coat at her elbow to anchor Vaughan. Sunshine's hum steadied the angles in her jaw.

The wind shifted. For one heartbeat, the smell of salt brightened into something sharper, cleaner, and Vaughan's eyes filled with tears.

"Grandmother?" she whispered.

No one answered. But the wind changed again, and with it the pressure at the edges of her mind. The thing above them had been waiting, calculating, patient as winter. It recognized what she was doing and altered itself in that subtle way predators do when the game changes but the hunger doesn't.

Something slid through the outward opening.

A vector, a seed. It wore the shape of a child, landing on the dock with the slightest wet slap of bare feet on wood. It was dripping, though not with river.

Flower's song snapped off. Sunshine's hum became a warning. Eli's hand went to the chalk at his ear, and he found nothing there.

The child lifted her face.

Vaughan's breath left her. It was her own face, eight years old, cut by a scar she did not have and never had, hair hacked short as if to be rid of the past it had held. The eyes were wrong. They were the pale, rinsed-out blue of sky bleached by noon, and there was nothing in them but weather.

"Don't," Sunshine said, stepping in front of Vaughan without thinking he had.

"Step back," Eli snapped, his voice a knife. "It will try to anchor itself to whichever of us calls it a name."

But the child was already looking beyond all of them—past the river, past the cranes, past the brittle city   to the line of the horizon. It smiled, small and private, like a girl who had found the door to the attic where her grandmother kept the trunk of letters no one was supposed to read.

"Thank you," she said to Vaughan. Her voice was Vaughan's voice at eight if she'd spent her childhood swallowing salt water. "I was so tired of being outside."

Vaughan's mouth went desert-dry. The door stuttered as if it were joining in. "Out," she managed. "This door is out."

The child cocked her head. "All doors are both," she said. "We only teach them manners."

Eli moved. He flicked chalk into a circle around the child, lines intersecting with quick, sure cuts. The child didn't stop him. She watched with fascination like a cat allowing a string to be pulled because it has already decided how it will tangle it.

Sunshine's hand pressed at Vaughan's back. "Close it," he breathed. "Close the hinge."

Vaughan tried. The wind held and then fought and then held again. The list in her pocket burned—not with fire, but with that clean brightness the wind had carried for a beat. Her grandmother's handwriting layered itself over Sunshine's scrawl in her memory. Doors outward. Names inward. Four people standing at the line on a dock that shouldn't have mattered and therefore did.

The child took a step to the edge of Eli's circle, toe bumping white chalk.

"Stop," Eli said. "Manners."

"Of course," the child said. She took a step back. And then she smiled the way Vaughan smiled when she had already made her decision and was indulging someone by letting them think they were part of it. "I will stand where you tell me."

The child lifted her hands the way children do when asking to be picked up.

Vaughan's heart stuttered because somewhere in the glow of memory and fear, a shape tried to fit herself around that gesture. The list in her pocket flared. The lines on her arms cooled further, ink pooling like iron filings tugged by a magnet.

"Don't touch it," Flower said. Every word was a stone dropped into a well.

"I wasn't going to," Vaughan said, then realized too late that she had planned to.

The child looked past her, to Sunshine. "You hum wrong," she said. "You rush. You always rush."

Sunshine flushed. "We didn't invite you," he said, the tremor in his voice audible only because Vaughan knew the map of his voice by now.

"You always invite me," the child said and reached very gently to touch the ribbon tied at Sunshine's wrist.

The ribbon blackened where its finger brushed it. It went from silk to a strand of night that had forgotten it had ever been matter. Sunshine flinched as if that small change had flicked him somewhere deep.

Eli's circle brightened like moonlit chalk. The child looked down, curious. "Manners," she echoed, delighted. "You speak them like laws."

"They are laws," Eli said tightly. "Here."

"Do you take your tea with salt?" the child asked, and something in the way she said the word tea made Vaughan taste frost again.

"Close it," Sunshine said, urgency rising. "Vaughan—"

"I am," she said. She was. But the hinge had become complicated. The wind tugged, and the bruise flexed.

A sound split the air. It was Flower.

Vaughan spun. Flower stood at the edge of the dock, the rosemary fallen, her face a readied blade. Eli had looped an arm around her shoulders from behind and dragged her back from the water. For a breath, Vaughan thought Eli was saving her from falling in.

Then she saw his other hand.

A knife. It was pressed just below Flower's ear.

Vaughan didn't breathe. Sunshine didn't. The child tilted her head and watched, as attentive as a scholar.

"Eli?" Sunshine said softly. Not disbelief. A request. Return. Choose.

Eli's jaw worked. His eyes found Vaughan's, and she expected to see void there. Instead, there was sorrow so thick it looked like anger. It looked like relief gone poisonous from being held too long.

"I told you," he said, voice steady in a way that would have sounded like kindness if not for the blade. "Extinction makes better speeches than vigilance."

"I don't—" Vaughan hated how her voice shook.

"Do you think you are the first?" he asked, not cruel. "Do you think the Order never understood that fire makes doors whether you open them or not? They chose theater over mathematics. They chose saints with blank faces over children who understood hinges."

With the knife against her skin, Flower didn't struggle. "Drive your point," she said. "And then listen to ours."

Eli's breath fluttered at her hair. "I am. We are out of time. I mean that precisely." His hand tightened. The knife kissed skin. A bead of blood gathered like a dark berry and did not fall.

"Eli," Sunshine whispered.

Vaughan felt the hinge quiver. The child's chalk circle dimmed. The list in her pocket burned cold. She moved without deciding to. The lines on her arms woke—heat this time, a swift hot thread—but she did not open. She took the heat and drove it into her calves, her shoulders, the place in her that knew how to cross a room before her mind had found the door.

"Don't," the child said, and for the first time, there was something like eagerness in her voice.

Vaughan lunged.

Eli was ready—of course he was. He'd watched her hands with chalk-dusted attention for days. He pivoted, dragging Flower with him as if she were a measure he was cutting to fit. Sunshine moved too, faster than anyone had the right to, intercepting not Eli but the line of the knife. He caught Eli's wrist, fingers digging, body a lever. The knife nicked deeper; Flower hissed but did not cry out.

The chalk circle around the child broke where Vaughan's heel scraped it. A thin line, a single hiss of broken manners.

The river sighed like something tired of pretending to be tame. The bruise dilated.

"Vaughan!" Sunshine shouted. "The door!"

She felt it. The hinge had reversed. Out had become in. Not all the way, but enough to change the problem from one of geometry to one of blood.

"Let her go," Vaughan said to Eli, her voice a quiet blade.

Eli's face was a ruin of emotion. "I can't," he said. "Because I will. Do you understand? I will. If I don't do it in my hands, the math will do it elsewhere. Better me than the unkindness."

"Unkindness," Flower said through her teeth. "Has never needed your help."

The child took a step toward the breach in the circle and placed its foot deliberately on the broken chalk. It did not leave a footprint. It left an absence.

"Stop," Sunshine said, and there was something in his voice Vaughan had never heard there—something old, and not all of it gentle. He let go of Eli's wrist with one hand long enough to slap the ribbon at his own wrist back over the path the child's finger had blackened. "Manners," he said, savage. "You don't touch what is tied."

The child paused. She looked at Sunshine as if noticing him for the first time. "Ah," she said, delighted. "You are the one who rushes. You are the one who will jump."

Sunshine's mouth went small and flat. "Not today."

"Today," the child said and took another step.

Vaughan had a choice. Close the door and lock the child in, risking that the hinge would pin Woolf-like at a choice she could not forgive herself for. Or open, fully outward, force whatever came through to leave.

"Burn." The thing in the sky breathed, no longer patient. It didn't bother with words in her ear now. It pushed them under her ribs like a commandment. "Burn and be hollow."

"Don't you dare," Flower said, and Vaughan realized the command was for both her and Eli.

"Let her go," Vaughan said again and took her hand off the idea of heat. She reached for the list in her pocket and pressed it flat against her chest until she could feel each of their names thudding against her sternum like small, stubborn hearts.

She took the horizon into her mouth like a word. She opened, outward, with everything she had that was not flame.

The wind slammed through them hard enough to knock the knife out of Eli's hand. It clattered. Flower wrenched herself free and shoved him backward with all the fury she had.

The child stepped into the breach in the circle as if stepping across a puddle.

Vaughan turned the hinge harder.

The wind howled, and the cranes groaned. The river reared up like it had been insulted. The sky above them tore no wider but turned very slightly.

The child's head snapped toward Vaughan. Her face did not change. Her eyes did. For the first time, something like fear crossed them thinly.

"Out," Vaughan said, and the word had weight because she made it in the shape of four names.

The child took a step backward. And another. And then it was at the edge of the dock, heels hanging over a river that had decided it could be an ocean for a few crucial seconds.

"Vaughan," Sunshine said in warning, awe, prayer.

"Out," Vaughan repeated, and the hinge in her chest flexed like a muscle she had not known she'd been training all her life.

The child smiled without humor. "All doors are both," she said again, then did something small and unforgivable:

It looked over Vaughan's shoulder. At Eli, who was no longer on the dock.

Vaughan spun.

Eli stood on the far side of the chalk circle, beyond where it had been broken, within reach of the child if the child had been in reach of anything. His face was calm again, not because it had forgotten sorrow but because it had made a ledger entry for it and closed the book.

"Eli," Flower said, ragged.

He looked at her, and for a moment, Vaughan thought she saw the man who had drawn sigils over their doors and told them that "good" was a thing they would craft themselves.

"I told you," he said quietly, and this time there was no anger around it at all. "I will."

He stepped forward and took the child's small, cold hand.

The wind faltered as if unsure which of two doors it now was.

"Eli—" Sunshine moved, but not fast enough this time.

The child's pale eyes flashed once like sun on mica.

Vaughan hurled all her will at the hinge. Outward, outward, outward—

—and Eli, with the gentleness of someone teaching a child that staircases are descended one careful step at a time, guided the small, wrong thing *in*.

The dock bucked. The chalk circle exploded outward into white dust. The wind died.

The bruise in the sky vanished. For half a heartbeat, the world was very quiet. Eli and the child were gone.

Vaughan staggered, breath scraped raw. Flower caught her. Sunshine stood frozen, ribbon bright against his wrist.

"Where—" Vaughan said, but the word broke.

"Inside," Sunshine whispered, voice thinned to wire. "He took it inside."

Flower's grip tightened on Vaughan's arm. "He made himself a door."

The river went flat again. The cranes remembered themselves. A gull wheeled and screamed because the world had to keep doing small, ordinary things or it would shake itself apart.

Vaughan swallowed hard enough to hurt. "We go after him," she said. "We find the hinge he made, and we pull him back through."

"Assuming he wants to come," Flower said, not to wound but to keep the math honest.

"He will," Sunshine said. "He's Eli."

Vaughan turned the list over in her pocket and felt their names like a map she had to learn fast enough to live. She pressed the horizon into her mouth once more and found, to her relief and terror, that it did not come as easily as before.

"Where do we start?" Flower asked.

Sunshine swallowed and lifted his head to the sky that had gone perfectly, offensively blue. He looked at the rebuilt astrarium circle he'd drawn on his card. The pointer spun once, then stopped dead. It pointed not north-northwest now, but to the floorboards beneath their feet.

"Down," he said hoarsely.

"Back to the sanctuary?" Flower asked.

Sunshine shook his head and knelt, pressing his ear to the plank. He went white. "No. Here."

Vaughan knelt with him and put her palm to the wood. For a moment, she felt nothing but old splinters and the damp breath of river. Then, a thrum—not like the astrarium, not like the song. Like a heartbeat too slow to be alive.

"Eli," she breathed.

"No," Sunshine said, and looked at her with eyes blown wide as night. "Vaughan . . . that's *you*."

Before she could pull her hand back, a sound rose from the dock like a whisper squeezed through a keyhole. It was her voice— younger, rawer, brittle with salt. It spoke from *beneath* the boards, from within the river, from the place where Eli and the child had gone.

"Promise me you won't leave."

Then the plank beneath Vaughan's hand splintered with a precise, surgical crack, and a small, pale hand—not Eli's, not the child's, *hers*—reached up through the ruin of wood and closed around Vaughan's wrist.

It was cold as iron. It pulled.

Everything else—the sky, the river, Flower's cry, Sunshine's hands slamming down to catch her—tilted.

Vaughan went down on one knee, breath punched free. Flower grabbed her shoulder with both hands and shouted her name in a voice Vaughan had never heard break before. Sunshine's fingers scrabbled for purchase on her coat, found the list in her pocket, and ripped it without meaning to—the paper tore like a promise suddenly too small.

"Hold her!" Flower screamed.

"I am!" Sunshine shouted back.

The hand in the dock tightened. The skin was hers, but it had no give. No warmth. It was a question that didn't care about the answer.

"Vaughan—" Sunshine said, and then his voice changed, went low and old again, not gentle. "Don't look at it. Look at me. Stay *here*."

Vaughan locked onto Sunshine's face and ignored the cold at her wrist, the way the dock kept whispering *promise me, promise me* in her own broken salt voice. She held his gaze until the blue of his eyes steadied into a horizon she could put her weight against.

"Doors outward," she said and pulled *back*.

For that single heartbeat, she felt it—a give, a slackening, a choice.

Then the hand in the wood squeezed, and the word outward tore in her throat and became *down*.

The dock split wider. Her center of gravity went with it.

Sunshine lunged, both arms around her, his mouth at her ear, a string of *no, no, no* like evidence. Flower cussed something blistering and threw her whole weight backward, feet braced against a mooring post, a human anchor swearing at the river.

"Let her go!" Flower roared into the opening.

From beneath the dock, from a darkness that did not echo and therefore had no bottom, Vaughan's own voice answered, impossibly calm:

"When you're hollow, I will step through."

The small hand pulled, gentle as tide, inevitable as debt, and the world tipped the last impossible inch—

—and Vaughan fell.

ACKNOWLEDGMENTS

ACKNOWLEDGMENTS

I am deeply grateful to everyone who has supported me in the creation of this book. First and foremost, I would like to thank my editor, **Shaina Clingempeel**, for her thoughtful feedback and for truly enjoying the editing process—she loved this book from the very beginning.

To my mom, **Sahar El**, thank you for your continued support and for helping me stay focused during the many late nights and weekends spent writing. Your patience and encouragement kept me going.

Finally, I would like to thank everyone who was eager to participate in my book tours and to all who provided moral support throughout this journey.

ABOUT THE AUTHOR

Avishai El is an international best-selling author of *I Made It Out* and *The Power of Why* Book Series. She is an award-winning Holistic Health Coach and internationally recognized Psychic Medium. Avishai is also the founder of **Avi Unfiltered**, where she merges spirituality, holistic medicine, and human empowerment to help people fulfill their purpose and achieve radiant wellbeing.

She has worked with women all over the world and has helped them lose weight, change their mental and emotional health, and reverse several diseases. Hospitals have entrusted her to be on record as a holistic nurse for cancer patients, and she has been featured among the top 10 wellness coaches in the world and leading experts in the field of neuroscience. A neuroadvocate and traumatic brain injury survivor, Avishai speaks, educates, and engages audiences to empower others on their healing journeys.

As a lifelong plant-based vegan, she actively promotes conscious living and sustainability. Her passion for protecting the planet and defending human rights fuels her mission to help people live freely and authentically. She comes from ancient ancestry and affirms that everyone has the right to life, liberty, and the pursuit of happiness.

Avishai is multilingual and currently studies her ancestral languages, including Latin, Moorish Latin (Modern-Day Spanish), Chaldean (Modern-Day Hebrew), Arabic, and Amharic. She also studies Astrology and medical research, and she regularly writes for **Brainz Magazine** as a UX copywriter for various businesses.

Black, white, and grey are her go-to colors, and the minimalist lifestyle brings her peace. When she's not writing, speaking, coaching clients, or running her many businesses, Avishai spends her time designing interiors, refining her innate makeup artistry, and exploring her creative passions — playing violin, singing, doing comedy, and much more.

ALSO BY AVISHAI EL

I Made It Out

The Man

Earthly Desserts

Dark Chocolate Love

Love Like Chocolate

www.ingramcontent.com/pod-product-compliance
Lightning Source LLC
Chambersburg PA
CBHW060324310726
48976CB00007B/2441